KISS OF DEATH

TEMPTING THE FATES BOOK ONE

ALICE WILDE

2nd Print Edition | Kiss of Death by Alice Wilde

©2023 Alice Wilde

For permissions contact:
alicewildeauthor@gmail.com

ISBN: 9798379214432

To the sacrifices we make for the ones we love.

CONTENT WARNING

Dear Reader,

Thank you for picking up this first book in my series, Tempting the Fates. Please be aware that this is a dark plot-heavy fantasy romance with multiple love interests. Each book will end on a cliffhanger, until the series is complete.

Please be aware that this series may not be suitable for all audiences, and certainly not for all ages. If you choose to continue, please be prepared to encounter some language, mental/physical abuse, murder, kidnapping, violent behaviors, the mention of non-con and attempted non-con (not by the love interests), death, violence, choking, voyeurism, mutilation, monsters, gods, revenge, redemption, heartbreak, and descriptions that may otherwise trigger you.

However, you will also find a great deal of wonderful and strange characters as well as angst, slow burn romance and eventual spice (this is not a fade to black series), and a cast of characters that is met and built slowly over the course of the series.

All this being said, there may be other triggers within the series that I have not listed. The journey will not be easy for our leading lady, but well worth it in the end.

Or so one can hope.

Now, shall we begin ...

Tempting the Fates?

Alice

HAZEL

S hutting the back door as quietly as possible behind me, I can't help but flinch as the latch slips into place. I pause, hardly daring to breathe as I wait for the sound of approaching footsteps from within.

Nothing.

Exhaling softly, the air rising in a steamy puff from my lips, I turn and make my way through the garden. The earth crunches beneath my feet, and I fight off a shiver as I wrap my arms around myself for warmth.

It shouldn't be this cold, not yet.

A glint of early morning sun catches my attention out of the corner of my eye, bringing me to a standstill. Frowning, I stop to look at the sunny marigolds my mother planted so long ago, their bright petals covered in glittering ice.

Glancing around the rest of the garden as the growing light brings it sparkling to life, I suddenly realize everything is blanketed in a fine layer of frost. My heart skips a beat in my chest as I gather my skirts to turn and dart down another path.

Reaching the vegetable patch, I sink onto my knees as I stare at the damage the frost has done. Browned and wilted herbs and vegetation are sprawled across the earth, their lives cut short far too soon. I can't help but feel like I've just lost several dear friends as I contemplate what to do next.

Merelda is going to kill me for this, if starvation doesn't take us sooner.

I know this isn't my fault, but I doubt my stepmother will see it that way. How was I supposed to know we'd get a frost this early?

Let alone at all.

Winter should still be a good two months away, and even then, it's rare that we get more than a few weeks of it.

Carefully gathering what is already too far gone of the vegetation, but still usable, into the makeshift basket of my skirts, I stand.

I'll have to make sure that I harvest whatever remains to be salvaged as soon as possible, but for now that'll have to wait.

Taking one last look at my poor plants, I turn to retrace my steps through the garden and continue on down the hill.

Reaching the chicken coop, I unlatch the door to let them out for the day, smiling at the soft cluck of their greetings as I scatter the remnants of my plants on the ground for them to enjoy. Ducking inside, I collect what few eggs I can find, tucking them into the gathering of my skirts.

"Come now, Florence," I sigh to the broodiest of our

2

hens as she chatters at me and fluffs up her feathers in frustration. "You know I can't very well leave you nesting with a chick-less egg, sweet girl. Besides, I'm a little short on breakfast supplies this morning."

I can't help but feel a little guilty as I slip a hand beneath her feathery skirts to extract the egg hidden within, but I know it's for her own good as well as it is mine.

We lost our rooster several months ago, and we've yet to go to market for another. I make a mental note to mention this yet again to Father.

Perhaps, if I can catch him alone before the others awake, he'll allow me to go to market by myself. Gods know the last thing he needs right now is more work, and I'd be all too happy to have a day out of the house for once.

The early morning sun warms my face as I leave the chicken coop. I'm already late to starting our morning meal, something my stepmother will certainly comment on if I don't hurry.

I can already see her frown forming in my mind, and I'll be lucky if a frown is all the punishment she doles out.

Racing back up to the house, I pray to the gods she hasn't woken let alone checked the kitchen yet. Breathing a small sigh of relief as I step into an empty kitchen, I'm grateful to see the fire is just starting to warm the cold stone.

Fighting off another shiver, I gently place this morning's bounty on the counter. I stare down at them for a moment, only now realizing that I'm still one egg short.

I suppose that means it'll be another egg-less breakfast for me. I'll have to make do with what remains of the staling bread I made several days ago and perhaps a bit of cheese. There might even be an apple or two tucked away on a back shelf if I'm lucky.

My stomach growls at the thought, only serving as a reminder that I'd been sent to bed hungry the night before after Merelda found the parsnip stew I'd made to be wanting. I hadn't even been allowed to stay up to greet Father on his return.

Turning, I slip into the small pantry to collect a rasher of bacon as well as my own meager breakfast. A bit of bread, some molding cheese, and a half-browned apple.

It'll have to do.

Taking a strip of cloth, I dampen it in some cool water before wrapping my bread in it and placing it on the stone by the fire to warm.

Scraping the layer of mold from my piece of cheese, I nibble on it between bites of gritty apple as I begin preparing breakfast for the rest of my family.

I reach for the cast iron skillet hanging above the counter, a present from my father to my mother on their wedding day.

A smile pulls at my lips as I run my hands along it. Her favorite place had been in this very kitchen, where the sunshine would pool at her feet as she hummed sweet songs while kneading dough.

Ghosts of the past keep me company as I place the skillet among the embers to warm it up while I begin cracking today's eggs into a bowl, whisking in what little milk we have left to thicken them.

Once, what now feels like a lifetime ago, this house had

been bathed in sunlight and warmth, the rooms full of laughter and love.

I'd been too young to fully understand the loss when my mother drew her last breath. She'd made me promise not to let her death harden me toward life, and I'd done my best to honor that wish.

It wasn't until Father introduced me to his new wife, Merelda, that I truly understood the weight of my mother's dying request. That I finally grasped just how much strength it would take to stay soft in a world hell-bent on breaking you.

Tears sting the backs of my eyes as I retrieve the skillet and carefully arrange thick cuts of bacon around the outer edge before returning it to the hot coals. My bread now softened and warm, I tear off small mouthfuls as I keep one eye on the sizzling pan. Flipping the bacon, I wait a moment before adding the egg mixture to the center of the pan as my mind wanders again.

Sometimes, I can't help but wonder how different life would be if Mother was still here. Now, I'm lucky if I get a few hours to myself, especially when father is away on business, which he almost always is.

He swears he's fine with the extra work, but I see the way his face has aged. He'd never admit it, but he's working himself to the bone trying to give my stepmother the kind of lifestyle she's accustomed to.

Unfortunately, I've been swept up into carrying that burden with him, though I'd never let him know as much. As soon as Father leaves, Merelda is quick to turn on me, ordering me about as she coddles her two *precious* sons.

The very thought of Amadeus and Cyprian is enough to have my stomach knotting, putting me off the rest of my breakfast.

Thankfully, I'm suddenly pulled from my spiraling thoughts by the sound of heavy feet on the stairs. Father, I'd know his footsteps anywhere.

These days, he's always in a hurry to leave, his feet falling a little too heavily on the wood. I can't help but wonder which client he'll visit next, and which of his beautifully bound books will pass into their hands.

Before, he'd let me read them as he painstakingly crafted their new covers. Now, I can hardly remember the last time I held a book.

Standing, I hurry to set the skillet on the counter to ready his breakfast. Reaching for a plate, I pause mid-reach as I hold my breath to listen closely for the soft footsteps of my stepmother, praying they don't follow him.

But they do. Of course, they always do.

Sighing, I quickly plate a bit of bacon and egg as well before turning toward the kitchen door.

"...really, Leoric. The way you slow your steps every time you must leave makes me wonder if you care for our family. Truly care," Merelda says, the high whine of her voice making me pause just inside the door.

"Don't say that, dearest," Father answers, his own voice low and gentle in contrast. "You know I care deeply for our family, and I always do my best to provide for you."

"And yet, you hesitate," Merelda sulks. "You know the lord will insist on a steep discount if you're even a moment too late on the delivery."

My heart sinks at this.

He's leaving, already? Father had promised me he'd be home for at least a week the last time he left.

Turning back to set the plate down on the counter, I hurry to bid Father farewell and perhaps end whatever disagreement the two of them are having. I know Merelda will be none too pleased to have me interrupt, but it's not as if she won't make me suffer for my father's absence anyway.

Wiping my hands on my skirts, I'm distracted by these thoughts as I near the door. So distracted that I don't hear the sound of approaching footsteps before it's too late.

The door swings open and I run straight into Amadeus, letting out a small squeak of surprise as I stumble backward. He catches me, his hand wrapping around my upper arm as a slow grin pulls at the corner of his lips.

"Hello, there," he says, his blue eyes darkening as he runs his free hand through his long golden hair, letting it briefly fall over his face for a moment before shaking it back. "I was just starting to wonder where you got to."

I open my mouth to demand that he unhand me at once, desperation tugging at my heart as I hear the front door open.

I have to say goodbye to Father. It's the one tradition we've managed to keep through the changing years. The one thing that helps me sleep at night when he's not here ... that and the prayers I send to the gods to watch over him as he travels. To bring him home safe to me.

I'm not sure how long he'll be gone this time, and I'd give almost anything for just a moment with him before he leaves. A few seconds is all I need to carry me through until he returns.

"Let me go," I demand, trying to force more steel into my voice than is there.

His grin only widens at this.

"I don't think so."

The way his eyes glint as he says this makes my stomach twist. His hand tightens around my arm, pulling me closer as if laying claim to me in doing so.

As if he could ever claim me.

Anger burns in my chest as I draw myself up to my full height, as small as that may be. Still, Amadeus has several inches on me, though not nearly enough for him to tower over me as I know he means to.

Meeting his gaze, I narrow my eyes.

"Let me go or I'll scream," I whisper. "You think they won't hear me from here?"

"So? It's not as if they'll take your word over mine."

The truth of his words stings, and for a moment, I forget my tongue.

"At least I don't have to cower behind my mother to get people to believe me."

"I do *not* cower," Amadeus hisses, his eyes flashing as he lifts his chin in an effort to appear taller.

A second too late, I bite my tongue as I realize I've only just made things worse for myself.

"I-I didn't mean—" I start, only to have my words cut short as he brings his other hand to my throat. My eyes widen in surprise as he shoves me backward, further into the kitchen, until my back is pressed against the cold stone of the wall and my arms are pinned behind me.

"Do I appear to be cowering now, sister?" he sneers, his eyes dropping lower. "Shame you aren't my type. The things I'd do to you. The things I'd have you *begging* me to do to you."

His fingers tighten around my throat as he shifts forward, and I can't help but gasp as I feel his wanton desire for me pressing into me. My cheeks burn hot as he smirks down at me, and I realize how little truly stands between us.

"...really, Merelda," comes my father's exasperated voice, drawing our attention toward the door, "Hazel will worry unless I bid her farewell."

"Nonsense," Merelda retorts with a cold laugh. "The girl is grown. You'll spoil her for other men with your constant doting. Come now, the carriage is ready. Here, take this, it'll do wonders for those dark circles of yours. Hurry now, you mustn't keep our clients waiting."

"It won't take but a moment."

Merelda stomps her foot, making a sound of annoyance. I can almost picture her pouting up at Father, arms crossed over her chest like an insolent child.

I can't help but wonder if she knows Amadeus is in here with me, or if she simply wants Father out of the house as quickly as possible so she can return to ordering me about.

"Is bidding farewell to your wife not enough for you, Leoric? Am I not enough for you?"

There's a sultriness to Merelda's voice that makes my stomach knot. Amadeus seems to sense my discomfort, his smirk growing as he presses me even flatter against the wall.

"Very well," Father sighs. "Hazel! I'm leaving, come say your goodbyes if you can hear me."

I start to answer, only for Amadeus to silence me as he shifts his hand from my throat to my mouth. His fingers dig into the hollows of my cheeks as the weight of Father's hopeful pause crushes my heart.

The silence drags on for several seconds as he awaits my reply, which never comes, thanks to the brute before me. Frustration causes tears to well in my eyes, even as I struggle to hold them back.

"See," Merelda says, "that girl is far too old for such silly little things. Come now, off you go."

Another second passes before I hear the heavy front door open and close. He's leaving, and without a farewell from me.

I writhe against Amadeus, but he just lets out a low chuckle as he leans in, his hot breath washing over my face.

"You know," he whispers, his hand moving to run his thumb along my lower lip, "now that we can be alone, perhaps you are my type after all."

Unable to stop myself, I take my chance and bite down on his hand.

Hard.

"You, *bitch*," Amadeus swears, stepping back from me to hold his hand up to inspect the bite. I can't help the small smile of satisfaction that overtakes me despite the sound of approaching footsteps.

Merelda throws open the door, her strawberry blonde

hair piled fashionably atop her head. She's young and beautiful, though the way her face suddenly twists at the sight of me makes that hard to see.

All it takes is one glance at her son's hand, and the broken skin in the shape of my teeth, to have her crossing the room. I open my mouth to try to explain, but her palm connects with my cheek, sending me stumbling to my knees as new tears spring to my eyes.

"How *dare* you disfigure him, you ungrateful little rat," she spits. "It appears I've been too lenient with you as of late. Finish breakfast, then see to mucking out the barn. Oh, and tend to the vegetables too, before the weeds choke them out."

Fighting back the tears, I swallow hard and nod once. The sooner I accept my punishment, the faster I can get away. Her eyes narrow on me, and for a moment, I worry that she's caught on to me.

But she turns and crosses to the kitchen door.

"And see that you serve meat with dinner today," she adds, pausing to glance back at me before finally leaving the kitchen.

I grimace, knowing that will mean losing yet another chicken with no way to hatch more anytime soon. Still, I waste no time scrambling to my feet, not even bothering to wipe the tears from my cheeks as I brush past Amadeus.

Tossing open the back door, I slam straight into my other stepbrother, Cyprian, nearly knocking us both down in the process. He catches me, steadying us both as he blinks at me in surprise.

11

"Hazel, what—" he slurs, his brow furrowing as he glances over me at Amadeus.

I pull away before he can finish his question, ducking around him and hurrying back into the garden.

My feet waste no time as they carry me over the path's crumbling stones and down the grassy hill to the wooden fence in desperate need of repair. The carriage has already passed, but it still might not be too late.

Leaping over the broken slats, I race along the grass to a large old tree that overlooks the small valley below and the end of the drive leading away from our house.

I make quick work of the low-hanging branches, straining to see the road at the bottom of the hill.

This is where I've always come to wave goodbye to Father, but today, there's no carriage for me to see off …

Just a cloud of dust that's already begun to settle back onto the road.

2

HAZEL

Wandering back to the broken piece of fence, I sigh and lean against it. Staring out at the trees and road beyond, my mind wanders, filled with worries about Father and his journey ahead.

I can't help but wish I could accompany him as I once did. Together, we'd travel the worn roads, laughing and sharing stories as we visited small villages and bustling towns where people were eager to buy from him.

It's been so long since I last left with him. Since we last shared a moment to ourselves.

My eyes still trained forward, I'm suddenly aware that I'm no longer alone. Tensing, I slowly glance over my shoulder to find Cyprian hovering a few steps away.

My nose wrinkles as he steps closer, the stench of alcohol wafting from him. The dark red of his nearly black hair falls rakishly around his face, sweat dotting his brow, as he peers at me through it. Dropping my gaze, I frown at his bloodied and bruised knuckles.

There's no doubt in my mind that he's been at the village tavern all night, fighting and drinking his time away.

"Are you alright?" he asks, his voice low.

My eyes lift to meet his, the sunlight sparkling in their sea-green depths somehow only improved by the dark circles forming beneath them. Despite his rough appearance, even I have to admit there's still some charm to the lopsided grin he gives me.

Perhaps it's because I know there's more behind those sad eyes of his than he'll ever let on.

I sigh, watching him as he comes to lean backwards against the fence. We say nothing for a long moment, though I can feel his eyes on me as my own return to the dirt road beyond.

"Hey, what happened back there?" he says, jerking his head toward the house.

I shrug. In truth, I'm not sure how to respond to him. His questions are too simple for the answers I'd have to give.

As the minutes drag on between us in silence, I can feel him growing impatient. Cyprian rolls his shoulders and neck, his movements straining the fence so that it groans under the added stress.

"Come on, you can tell me," Cyprian presses, nudging me in an attempt to draw my eyes back to him.

Annoyance flares to life in me as I turn toward him, ready to give him an earful.

Until I meet his eyes.

The snappy words die on my tongue as I swear that I

see genuine worry and care burning within his gaze. For a moment, he almost looks sober as he stares down at me.

Biting my cheek, I find myself suddenly on the verge of telling him the truth. Of giving life to the words that I've long since buried deep within myself.

Cyprian and I have never been close, he's always preferred keeping to himself, and I'm not sure why I feel the urge to spill my guts to him. To tell him how miserable I've been since his mother and brother came into my life.

How hard it has been not to grow hateful as the years passed. How nothing has been right in my life since they entered it and began changing everything.

At first, it had meant bidding farewell to the stable boy, my sole childhood friend, and his mother who had taken over as our cook and housekeeper after mother died. Then, it was being moved to the smallest room at the back of the house. The one with a broken window that let the chill in during Winter and the bugs in the rest of the year.

Next came the chores. The rising before dawn to tend to the tasks Merelda deemed too lowly or too womanly for her own sons.

This was only half of it, and I would have borne it all with a smile for the sake of Father's happiness, but then she took him away from me too ... and I was forbidden from traveling with him again.

My father fought her on this, but she wouldn't budge, claiming that having a young woman with him invited scandal upon us and could ruin *her* reputation, not to mention his.

So, it was settled, and I was forced to remain here under

her watchful eye. Utterly and completely alone in the world, with only my cruel step-family to torment me, should they remember I even existed.

Slowly, my father's monthly trips turned into more and more, spanning greater lengths of time as he was forced to travel further to accommodate Merelda's expensive tastes.

Now, most weeks slip by without him being here. My days spent missing him as I tend to the endless chores Merelda finds for me.

With this unexpected trip, I'm starting to worry that he won't return before my birthday. I was being childish, as my stepmother was all too willing to remind me, for wanting him to be here to celebrate the day rather than out providing for the family.

But I know that without him, the day will slip by without mention.

Perhaps I am selfish for wanting what I lost the moment he brought Merelda into our lives. For longing for the days when it was just the two of us.

Had I known then just how precious those moments were, I would have hung on a little tighter and fought a little harder to keep them from slipping through my fingers. Now, all I want is just one more day spent with Father as it had once been.

A single tear slips down over my cheek, startling me back to the present. I hadn't realized the depth of my heartache until now.

My eyes shift to Cyprian, who's still watching me. For a moment, there's a strange awareness in his own gaze.

The haze of alcohol that I've become all too familiar

with rises as he turns and lifts a hand toward me. Flinching, I see the pain on his face at my reaction.

His hand freezes just inches from my face as though he's finally realized what he was about to do.

"Hazel," he says, his voice a rough contrast from the softness of his eyes.

"Well, isn't this sweet."

Cyprian drops his hand, though I fear it's too late. Looking past him, I watch as Amadeus steps into view. He smirks as he glances between me and his younger brother.

Clapping a hand on Cyprian's shoulder, it takes a second for me to realize he's misread the situation and mistaken my tears as his brother's doing.

"How did you do it?" Amadeus questions, though his eyes never leave me. "I suspect it wasn't hard, she always does seem to be on the brink of tears as it is. Perhaps you should try smiling sometimes. Don't you think she'd be prettier if she smiled for us, brother?"

"There's nothing worth smiling about when you're around."

His eyes flash at my words, spat at him in disgust over his suggestion that I smile more. As if he and his family aren't the reason that I find it harder and harder to do so.

I watch as his knuckles whiten on Cyprian's shoulder, wondering what punishment for me he's coming up with in his mind.

"Mother was right about you," Amadeus sneers. "You really are nothing but an ungrateful bitch. Someone really should teach you a lesson about your place in this world."

"If that's the case, then I'd prefer to be taught that by

17

someone who doesn't think higher of themselves than they are."

In a blink, Amadeus has pushed past Cyprian, the force of his sudden movement causing him to stumble drunkenly backward to the ground. I straighten, refusing to give in to fear as I lift my eyes to meet his furious gaze.

He shoves me back against the fence, grinning as it hits the small of my back, causing me to let out an involuntary grunt of pain.

"Careful, girl," he warns, stepping closer. "Your father isn't here to save you. Perhaps it's time I finally show you the only thing you're really good for."

Amadeus reaches for me, his fingers dipping below my neckline as he presses his body to mine. I go still as he yanks open the lacing at my bust, his other hand shifting to my skirts as he jams his knee up between my legs. My mind is racing, but my body remains in shock.

He's going to get what he wants, and I'm too scared to stop him.

Then, just as suddenly as it all started, it stops as a large hand yanks Amadeus back from me.

"Come now, Deus," Cyprian says, his words far more slurred than they were just a few minutes ago. "Where's breakfast? I need food, and perhaps some wine. No, *definitely* more wine."

Amadeus glares at him for a moment, before glancing back at me as he shifts uncomfortably on his feet, and I only just now realize he's holding his cock in his hand ... or at least, what little of it I can see.

"Have you not had enough already, *brother*?" he hisses.

Cyprian snorts at this.

"I wasn't aware there was such a thing as enough wine," he answers. "Besides, isn't it her job to make sure we're fed? The longer we stay out here, the longer until we get a good meal."

For a breath, I don't think Amadeus is going to give me up so easily, but then he relents. As if on cue, his features change as he dons a mask of boredom. With a snort of his own, he shoves himself back into his pants, and I'm careful not to sigh in relief or do anything to draw his unwanted attention back to me.

Running his hand through his long blonde hair, he straightens out his clothes before turning his back to me. Slinging an arm around Cyprian's shoulders, he starts off toward the house, dragging his brother along with him without a final word or glance my way.

Only Cyprian does look back, his eyes meeting mine for a split second. He gives me a strange look, his eyes softening toward me in a way I'm far from used to.

I can't help but worry that he's only just realized I'm a woman, something his brother wasted no time acknowledging since the first time we met. Did he save me from his brother because he actually cares about me, or was it simply because he couldn't stand by and watch?

Pushing away from the fence as soon as the two of them are out of sight, I hiss in pain as I stare down at my palm.

A single splinter of wood sticks out from it, a small droplet of blood already beading on the surface. Shuddering, I pull it from my hand before rubbing my sore lower back.

Cyprian was right about one thing, unfortunately. I had better hurry back to finish preparing breakfast before I'm left with any more bruises. Still, I pause for just a moment to glance back over my shoulder.

Father is long gone, but I still find myself hoping for some sign that he will be fine ... That he will return in time.

Instead, I'm left with an empty road. Letting out a single sigh, I move away from the fence.

I should know better by now than to hope the gods hear my pleas.

3

HAZEL

The days drag by as I wait for Father to return, the bruises on my back from the caning I got the first night after he left still healing.

She's always been good at making sure the marks of my punishments were never visible to the naked eye.

I grimace in pain as I carry water back from the well at the bottom of the hill to fill a bath for Merelda. Just one of the seemingly endless tasks she's found to fill every waking moment.

And, should I pause to catch my breath? She'll be at my heels, complaining about my laziness as she tacks on a dozen more chores for me to finish before bed.

After the incident in the kitchen, Merelda seems hell bent on making my waking life as miserable as possible. I have no choice but to go about my chores in silence, praying for Father's quick return ... or something, anything else to distract her.

Exhausted, I drag myself to bed later and later each

night. Not only have the chores taken their toll on me, but Amadeus has made it obvious he intends to corner me.

I won't allow it, no matter how tired I may be.

Evading his advances has become a constant part of my day, and I often find myself on edge as I peer around corners and press myself into shadows in the very house that was once my safe haven.

Thankfully, the makeshift bar I've managed to place across my door has kept me safe at night.

Waking in the morning, my eyelids are heavy as I prepare for the day ahead. It's becoming harder and harder to drag myself from bed.

Going about my morning chores, I do my best to blend in with the stones of the walls. If I were more fortunate, my step family would simply forget that I existed. Yet, that seems the furthest thing from Merelda and Amadeus's minds.

Cyprian, on the other hand, seems to be embracing the distraction. I've barely seen more than a glimpse of him since breakfast the morning my father left.

Now, days have passed since he last returned home, much to Merelda's displeasure. While her words are always sharper toward me when she paces the floor in worry over her youngest son, her hands are not.

It's only when the steady thrum of her heels against the wooden floor stops that I'm jolted from my thoughts, my ears prickling from the sudden silence.

"Cyprian, dear, is that you?" Merelda calls, worrying the ring on her hand as she peers out at the front entryway.

I tense where I am across the room, slowly rising from

the floor I've spent the last few hours tirelessly scrubbing. There's a long pause before Cyprian steps into view, looking much worse for the wear than usual.

His eyes find me before quickly darting away ... just as they have each time he's returned home since Father left.

Collecting my things, I move silently through the room in an effort to leave them both behind as quickly as possible. I swear I can feel his eyes on me, even as I keep my own trained on the floor.

"Where on earth have you been?" Merelda asks, her voice dry.

I pause, just outside of Merelda's peripherals as I wait for him to answer, not wanting to draw her attention to me. Daring a look at him, I find him watching me, not so much as sparing a glance at his mother.

My heart thuds in my chest as I quickly drop my eyes again.

"Cyprian, answer me at once!"

Again, he says nothing, this time turning to disappear down the hall even as Merelda hurries to the doorway to stare after him.

I watch as Merelda worries her lower lip between her teeth until we're both startled by the slamming of his bedroom door. It's obvious where he's been, and undoubtedly, where he'll soon be again.

He'll change his clothes, leaving the torn and bloodied garments behind before disappearing again. If she's lucky, he might stay long enough to grab a bite to eat from the kitchen, but it's unlikely.

"That boy," Merelda mutters to herself before glancing

back at me. Her eyes narrow as she snaps, "You, girl. I expect you to tend to his garments. I want them soaked and mended by morning. Bring him something to eat too, quickly now."

I swallow back any response I might have to this, and simply nod once.

"I still expect these floors to be shining before you go to bed. The chicken coop needs cleaning as well, and the pantry seems to have collected ants. Oh, and I think we'll have a chicken pot pie for dinner."

I bite my tongue at this. Mentioning that we have but a few chickens left will only send her into a fit of rage. She watches me for a second longer before disappearing into a room down the hall, finally leaving me alone to tend to go about my day.

I listen for the sound of the lock, letting a small smile form on my face when I finally hear it. She won't be out for hours, if not the rest of the day.

I know what she keeps in there, and the strange mind-altering mixtures she likes to imbibe on days like this.

These are the days I like best. The ones where Amadeus is nowhere to be found, and I'm left alone to work without Merelda scrutinizing my every move.

Setting my cleaning supplies down in the kitchen, I wash my hands before putting together a small plate of leftovers and a mug of water. I stare down at the items on the counter, dreading the next part of my task.

Perhaps, I can just leave it all outside Cyprian's door.

Satisfied with my plan, I quietly make my way upstairs.

Pausing outside Cyprian's door, I frown as I hear a strange sound from within.

I open my mouth to say something, but think better of it, instead bending to place the plate of food on the floor. Only, the door swings open before I can.

"Hazel," Cyprian says in a sharp whisper. "Come in."

I hesitate, still half bent over as I try to think of a reason to refuse. Straightening, I start to say something, but stop as my eyes fall to his bare chest.

"What happened?" I gasp.

"Please, not here," he says, his eyes darting toward the stairs as he steps to one side and reaches to pull me inside his room, quickly shutting the door behind him.

"Who did this to you?"

He laughs sharply at this before it turns into a cough.

"*I* did this to me," he answers once he can speak again, brushing past me to throw open his wardrobe and pull out a new shirt.

I can't help but stare at the bloody lacerations and bruises that litter his torso. If I didn't know better, I'd almost swear he'd been beaten to within an inch of his life at some point in the past few days.

"Tell me, honestly. What happened?"

Cyprian sighs, his shoulders tensing for a moment before he drops his head in defeat and slowly turns to look at me. Our eyes meet, and for a moment I see that same dark ocean of sadness within them that I've felt for so long.

"I got in a fight, that's all. Nothing new."

"But who would do this to you?"

"Look, I wasn't lying when I said I did this to me,"

Cyprian answers. "I picked the fight. I *wanted* to fight. I wanted to feel pain."

I blink at him. Of course, him getting into fights isn't anything new, but I've never seen him like this.

As far as I know, Cyprian doesn't lose his fights.

"Why?"

His eyes pull away from mine as he turns back to the wardrobe.

"Because," he starts, "because I deserve as much. I deserve to feel what my family has put you through. What I haven't been man enough to protect you from."

I can hardly believe what I'm hearing as he grabs a clean pair of pants and tosses them onto the bed. I watch as he starts pulling on the new shirt.

"Wait," I say, and he stops mid-movement. "You'll ruin the shirt before you even get it buttoned in that state."

Cyprian cocks his head slightly to the side, his brow furrowing as he lifts his gaze to meet mine. I look away nearly as quickly as I turn to set the plate down on the nightstand.

Crossing to him, I pull a clean rag out of my apron pocket and dip it in the mug of water before gently pressing it to one of the lacerations on his chest. He doesn't so much as hiss in pain, the slight flare of his nostrils the only indication that I'm causing him any discomfort.

Cyprian doesn't speak, choosing instead to watch in silence as I carefully clean the fresh and dried blood from his upper body.

"There, that should do for now," I say, stepping back to

take one last look at him. His skin, while still bearing the marks of his fight, is free of blood.

As my eyes travel over him, I can't help but admire the beauty of his form. It's not altogether unlike the statues I've seen in larger towns and cities. He's taller than Amadeus, his body well-proportioned and honed to fight.

It's only as my eyes drop lower, tracing the lines of his abs that I suddenly look away. My cheeks burn with heat as I realize what I've just been doing.

"Thank you," Cyprian says, stepping closer and reaching out to gently lift my chin with one finger. I stare up into his eyes for a long moment before pulling away.

"I-It was nothing."

"Hazel—"

I don't stay long enough to hear what he says as I rush from the room, shame and heat coloring my face.

I finish the rest of my chores with a haphazard disregard for my own thoroughness, only daring to venture nearer the house again when I hear Merelda shouting.

Ducking behind a tree, I watch as Cyprian exits the front door, yanking his arm out of his mother's grasp as she desperately tries to stop him from leaving.

"Cyprian, get back here this instant! I'm warning you, if your father hears about this—"

"My father?" Cyprian laughs bitterly, whirling on her. "*My* father is dead, or have you forgotten that already?"

Merelda doesn't answer for a moment as she takes a menacing step toward her son.

"You will not speak to me like that," she hisses. "I am your mother, whether you like it or not. You'll never understand what I've had to do for you—"

"No, you're right about that," Cyprian cuts her off, shaking his head in disgust. "I'll never understand."

With that, he turns and storms out of sight as Merelda screams after him to no avail. When it's clear he's not coming back, she suddenly grows calm. Her face blanks as she brushes back several loose strands of hair before turning back into the house.

The door slams shut, and I all but breathe a sigh of relief.

My relief is short lived though as I make my way down to the chicken coop, only to remember what she's ordered for dinner. Of all the things I have to tend to, butchering is the one task that never gets any easier.

I understand it's a necessity of life, but it's been harder since I've had to start butchering the hens. They were raised for eggs, and I'd always thought of them as my friends, not to be eaten.

Pulling a handful of scraps that I'd collected while cleaning the ants from the pantry earlier from my apron pockets, I scatter them across the ground. My eyes trained on the single piece of apple lying in the midst.

This was how I chose which chicken would be killed to feed my step family, by leaving their lives up to fate.

The hens cluck gratefully, and I watch them tearfully

28

until they've finished every last morsel before ushering them into the coop for the night.

Tears blind my eyes as I sink to my knees in front of the hen who'd eaten the bit of apple.

"I-I'm so sorry," I choke, gently reaching out to pet her before tucking her into the crook of my arm. "I'm so, so sorry, Florence."

Leaving the coop, I walk slowly back up to the house as I continue to pet Florence and whisper sweet memories of our time together. My heart is breaking in my chest, but I refuse to let it show as I tell her everything that I love about her.

Entering the kitchen, I set Florence down on a wooden block.

"Here you go, sweet girl," I say, pulling out a few black-berries I'd plucked earlier and placing them in front of her so that her back is to me.

Florence excitedly pecks at the berries as I turn to grab a sharpened knife. Gathering my courage, I wait until she's nearly done before quickly and cleanly cutting her life short.

I haven't even set the knife down before the door to the kitchen is thrown open, Merelda now filling the space.

"Forget dinner," she says. "I have a headache and will be retiring to my rooms. Amadeus won't be back until late, and gods know when Cyprian will return."

"But I've already killed one of the chickens," I stammer.

Merelda gives me a look of disgust.

"And? What use is it to me now?"

With that, she spins on her heel, the door swinging shut behind her.

I feel like the air has been sucked out of my lungs as I crumple forward. Bracing myself against the counter, I let my tears fall as I mourn Florence's death, my heart breaking into pieces.

When I can finally breathe again, I straighten, wiping the tears from my eyes as I set to work making sure Florence's life wasn't taken in vain. They may not want dinner, but that doesn't mean I'll allow her to go to waste.

They will eat what they've sown, whether they want to or not.

4

HAZEL

The day finally drawing to a miserable end, I exit the kitchen through the back door, tomorrow's meal planned and prepped. With Merelda and her sons gone for the night, I am determined to make the most of what little time I have to myself.

I make my way down a small path, the fading sunlight filtering through the trees in warm golden rays, despite the chill of the day. Reaching a small clearing, I smile as I gaze upon Father's workshop.

Our workshop.

It sits empty, the shutters pulled, and the fireplace long gone cold. I can't even remember the last time I was here, as much as I've yearned to be.

This is the one place my step family knows never to venture into.

Better yet, they *can't* venture into.

I'll be safe here, at least for the several stolen hours I've suddenly found myself with. Glancing around, I kneel to

31

wrestle a loose stone out of place before reaching in to pull out a small golden key.

Quickly replacing the stone, I hurry to unlock the door, throwing it open as a smile spreads across my face. Even in the darkness, I can just make out the bottles of ink, the smell of parchment and wood, and the lingering scent of smoke, oil, and turpentine.

Scrambling to light several lanterns, I finally close the door as I sigh deeply to myself.

I give myself a moment to take in the room now that it's been made somewhat more visible. From the beautiful pigments and oils from far-off cities to the brushes and quills that fill small jars and lay scattered about everywhere in perfect chaos. Candle stubs litter nearly every surface, solidified wax dripping from the edges of easels and shelves alike.

For the first time in what feels like forever, I feel like I'm home.

My eyes land on a blank canvas already set up on one of my father's easels. My fingers itch, and I'm forced to clasp my hands together to keep them from worrying a hole in my skirts.

I don't have enough time. It would be foolish to try.

Still, I can't quite convince myself not to as the canvas continues to call my name.

It's easy work coaxing a fire to life, the workshop taking on a whole new life in its soft orange glow. I know it's not the best lighting for painting, but it'll have to do.

Throwing open a nearby window, I shiver as a chilly gust of wind whips around me, rustling several nearby papers before settling. The forest outside has grown dark with the setting of the sun, and for a moment I swear the shadows take on a life of their own.

Shaking my head at the silly notion, I turn back to prepare my palette. Thankfully, Father has already prepared and stored most of the colors I need in carefully labeled animal bladders. Though, I suppose the very fact they're laying here untouched means he hasn't been around enough to use them.

Poking several of the bladders with a bone pin, I squeeze what I need of the oil paints within onto a palette. I'll have to mix several other colors later, but this will do for now.

Returning to the easel, I set my palette down and open a small jar of linseed oil and another of turpentine.

Staring at the blank canvas before me, I'm reminded of the days I once spent here. Days spent at Father's side as he taught me how to read and write, and finally to create. He'd even let me help him with several of his projects as my skills had grown.

Reaching for a brush, I take a deep breath before letting it out slowly. There's no denying that this is the most content I've felt in days.

Years, even.

Pushing aside all the worries and troubles of my life, I clear my mind as I coat my brush and lift it to the canvas. It isn't long before the world has melted away around me, and I find myself lost in my art.

In the past, if I'd found myself here with a few hours to spare, I'd spend my time illustrating one of the heavy tomes my father had been commissioned with, but not today. Today, I take my time as I dip my brushes into the smooth oils, swift strokes of color gradually coaxing an image onto the canvas.

A strange forest begins to take shape beneath my brush, a small cottage sitting tucked away within the dark trees as candlelight flickers warmly in the windows. It's a surprisingly cozy looking place, despite the darkness that surrounds it.

I'm wholly lost in the process as the scene continues to take on a life of its own. My whole body moving in rhythm with the canvas as I feel a smile tug at the corner of my mouth.

Until I suddenly become aware of another's presence.

Turning to look over my shoulder, I let out a startled cry as I find Cyprian leaning in the open doorway.

"How long have you been there?" I ask.

"A while. Please, don't stop on my account."

I hesitate before placing a few shaky strokes on the canvas. Glancing back at Cyprian, his eyes remain soft as he meets my gaze. He offers me a small smile that only serves to put me further on edge.

Did I give him the wrong impression earlier?

How is he even here? Only Father and I have keys to this workshop, not even Merelda was allowed one.

So, how is it that he's come to be here?

Belatedly, I realize that in my eagerness to paint again, I'd forgotten to lock the door. He must have seen the light from the open window and ...

"Why are you here?" I suddenly blurt out, relieved that

34

my voice comes out frosty enough to take Cyprian by surprise.

He blinks, but doesn't answer. Despite the way I narrow my eyes at him, he pushes away from the doorway and takes a step inside.

My heart races as his eyes move across the room, taking everything in before finally landing on my own work. I'm half tempted to shield my painting from him as he cocks his head to the side to get a better look.

And yet, I don't.

He moves further into the room, coming to stand just behind my shoulder as he quietly looks at my art.

"It's not finished—"

"It's stunning."

I blink in surprise. I'm not sure what to make of his words, let alone whether or not to believe them. His voice is gentle, but I can't help feeling wary of trusting him. Not after everything his family has put me through.

Even after what he told me earlier.

Could this all be some kind of trick? Some means of getting me to put my guard down?

I watch him warily as he leans over me to study the painting closer, the heat of his body so close to my own making me shift uncomfortably on my feet. This sudden change in our dynamic is unsettling, to say the least.

Not that I don't prefer whatever *this* is compared to his usual detachment or his brother's downright cruelty. Still, I keep a wary eye on him as he reaches around me to lift my art up into the light, careful to avoid touching the wet paint.

His body is all but pressed up against me from behind,

the thundering of my heart only drowned out by the sudden sound of heavy footsteps just outside the workshop.

Cyprian lets out a low curse as he sets my painting back down on the easel. Before I have a chance to react, he's already spun me around to face him, his hands wrapping around my upper arms as his jaw hardens.

Gone is the softness I've recently glimpsed in him, replaced with the cold aloofness I've come to expect of him.

"Cyprian," I hiss, just as Amadeus suddenly appears in the doorway behind us. His eyes narrow on us as he takes in the scene. Then, the corner of his mouth twitches, his lip curling up in sneer as he steps wordlessly into my father's workshop.

My stomach twists as he closes the door behind him, sealing me in here alone with the two of them ...

"I'm impressed, brother," Amadeus says, his eyebrow arching. "You actually managed to corner the little mouse ... And in the one place that Mother won't think to look. Well done, indeed."

Fear fills me as I glance from Amadeus to Cyprian.

His eyes have grown dark, trained on his brother, and it's only now that I realize what a fool I've been.

I never should have allowed myself any softness toward him. I never should have gone to his room. Never should have done anything to draw his attention to me.

The moment he appeared in the doorway, I should have known no good would come of him being here. I should have made him leave.

Instead, I let him trap me here.

Amadeus takes a leisurely step closer, his eyes on me as the corner of his mouth drags upwards into a smirk.

I may not have any true experience when it comes to men, but even I can sense the desire in his look. My gut twists as I glance past him toward the door. Even if I were to escape Cyprian's grip, I'd never make it past his brother.

I'm well and truly trapped.

Cyprian's fingers tighten around my arms, and I let out a small hiss of pain. Instantly, his grip loosens, and without a word he releases me as he turns toward his brother. Taking a step forward, he places himself directly between me and Amadeus.

"Yeah, I did catch her in here, and now I think *you* should go."

Amadeus blinks, obviously taken aback by his brother's words. He tilts his head to the side as he looks Cyprian over.

"And why is that?" he asks.

"You know Mother will want to know she has access to this place. We shouldn't delay telling her."

Amadeus scoffs at this, making my stomach twist even tighter as any hope that had sprung to life in my chest withers and dies. He won't be so easily swayed to leave this time.

"You must be three sheets to the wind if you think I'm not going to take full advantage of the situation first," Amadeus says. "No, no I don't think I'll leave just yet. In fact, I daresay, Mother needn't know anything about this. This can be our little secret."

Cyprian shifts slightly at this, subtly tucking me further

behind him as he cracks his neck to one side and squares off his shoulders.

If I didn't know any better, I'd almost think that he's trying to protect me from his brother. Hiding me from his hungry gaze.

"We shouldn't be in here," Cyprian presses. "If we were caught—"

"Why the hell should I care about that?" Amadeus snorts. "I'm not passing up an opportunity like this again."

Closing the distance between him and his brother, he reaches around Cyprian as if to drag me out from behind him.

Again, Cyprian shifts to block him.

Even from here, I can see the way Amadeus' eyes flash with annoyance. He's not used to anyone stopping him from getting what he wants.

"What are you playing at now, little brother?" Amadeus demands, glaring up at Cyprian as his fury seems to grow to match his lust. "Have you suddenly taken an interest in the little mouse? Fine. We can both have our fun with her, but *I'm* taking her first."

I clench my teeth together in an effort to stop myself getting sick as I worry that there's no escape for me from this.

"No," Cyprian growls, his fists clenching at his side.

Amadeus narrows his eyes up at Cyprian before suddenly throwing his head back, cold laughter spilling from him.

"You amuse me, brother, but there's no way I'm going to

allow you to be the one to ruin her. *That* pleasure is all mine."

"Touch her," Cyprian says, the words low and threatening, "and it'll be the last thing you do."

Quiet fills the workshop as the smile slips from Amadeus' face as the two of them stare one another down. Any humor that Amadeus felt has left him as his face slowly turns pink with rage.

Cyprian's jaw hardens as he pulls himself up even straighter, staring down at his older brother. This is all it takes to finally set Amadeus off as he suddenly swings a fist at Cyprian.

That's all that Cyprian needs, too, as he dodges and launches himself at Amadeus.

A startled shriek escapes me as the two of them come barreling toward me. I just barely manage to dive out of the way, but I can't say the same for my painting as Amadeus crashes into it.

Disappointment curls around my heart as I look at the smudged paint, my hard work all ruined. My paints and brushes are sent flying to the floor as Amadeus scrambles to throw himself at Cyprian again, but I barely notice them. Fighting back my tears, I crouch and grab the painting from the floor.

I can't seem to tear my eyes from it as the two continue to fight, jars smashing to the floor as paper and ink are strewn about the workshop. Slowly, I return to the present as I hear something else. Faintly at first and then growing ever louder.

Turning toward the window, I race over to it, leaning

out into the cold dark night. Sure enough, it's a sound that I've spent many sleepless nights waiting for.

I can't help but smile, even as I glance back at the destruction behind me.

A carriage on the drive this late at night can only mean one thing.

Father is home.

5

HAZEL

Spinning on my heel, I duck past Cyprian and Amadeus, several glass bottles smashing to the floor as I hurry from the workshop before either of them can stop me. I hear their shouts behind me as I hurry along the path back toward the house, kicking up a small storm of dust as I go.

Turning the front corner of the house, I can't help but smile as I watch Father's carriage slow to a stop.

"Father!" I shout, just as Merelda appears at the door, her face souring the moment she sees me.

"Hazel—"

But before she can send me off to my room or to tend to some chore that surely doesn't need my immediate attention, the door to the carriage opens. Father steps out, and I fling myself into his arms, his laugh vibrating through me.

Behind me, I can feel Merelda's annoyance boring into me that I'm the first to greet him, but it only makes me savor the moment that much more. Father's arms wrap around me, and my heart warms with joy.

"I've missed you so," I whisper. "I'm so glad you're back."

"I missed you too, daughter," Father says with a chuckle. "Besides, tomorrow is a very special day that I wouldn't miss for the world."

"What day is that?" I ask.

"Surely, you haven't forgotten your own birthday," he says with another small chuckle.

I take a step back, blinking in surprise. I'd completely forgotten.

Merelda suddenly appears, brushing me to one side without so much as a glance in my direction. I watch as she fusses over him, catching his face in both hands as she coos at him, assuring him that every day without him here has been worse than the last.

I frown as I take another step back, melting into the background as I watch the two of them. Beside her, Father looks pale and worn, as though he raced back home without stopping to sleep.

Even his eyes are dull, lacking the sparkle that they once always had.

"Hazel, dear, I know it's late," Merelda says with a sigh, "but would you please help with dinner? Your father looks famished, and I'm sure he could use a bit of fresh air after being stuck in the carriage all this time."

Her tone is sickly sweet, yet another act for Father's sake. I could almost laugh aloud at the way she said help, as if I won't be the only one tending to everything and making sure there's a warm meal for them to enjoy.

I glance up at him, hating the way he smiles down at her. The fondness on his face though is enough to have me nodding to my stepmother as I turn and disappear into the house.

Thankfully, the kitchen is empty as I step into it.

Sighing, I reach to pull my apron off the hook by the door. Tonight, I don't mind the solitude the kitchen has to offer, even as late as it is.

Setting about slicing an onion, I even welcome the tears it brings to my eyes. Nothing can ruin the joy I feel at having Father home. He remembered and returned in time for my birthday, and that alone is better than any present he could have brought me.

I let this happiness carry me through as I finish preparing the chicken from earlier, feeling somewhat better that it'll be Father who is nourished by her sacrifice rather than just my step family.

By the time the fragrant smell of roasted chicken and herbs fills the kitchen, I'm actually excited about dinner. With the table set and our meal almost ready, I hang my apron back up.

Dusting off my skirts, I take the roast chicken into the dining room, unable to keep a smile from spreading across my face.

Everyone is already seated, even Cyprian and Amadeus, each wearing clean outfits as they glare at each other from across the table.

From the tight expression on Merelda's face, she's

43

already impatient for the meal to be over and done with. Father, however, smiles at me, giving my arm a little squeeze as I serve him first.

"It smells heavenly, Hazel," Father compliments before taking a bite.

"Tell us, Leoric, how were your travels?" Merelda asks, drawing his attention away from me and the meal.

I serve the rest of my family, avoiding the looks Cyprian and Amadeus shoot me, before taking my own seat. Picking at the food on my plate, I listen quietly as Father regales us with tales of his trip. From the dusty inns he stayed at and the strange characters he met along the road to the fine manor of his latest client, he spares no detail.

Merelda pretends to listen, her gaze mostly trained on her plate as she makes small sounds of absentminded acknowledgment at regular intervals. I do my best to ask the questions that she fails to.

Watching him, I can't help but feel that there's a new pinch to his eyes. A new tightness around his mouth. Try as I might, I can't seem to write it off as him just being travel weary.

"Next week, I'm expected back at the coast," Father says, pushing his empty plate away. "Lord Savvas has commissioned three new books. All tales of the gods to be illustrated, and I'm afraid I'll be quite busy for the foreseeable future."

"That's great news," I say, perking up. "I'd be happy to help you illustrate them, Father."

"I may just have to take you up on that," he says, giving me a tired smile as he pushes his chair back. "However, if you will all excuse me, I find that my travels have worn me quite thin."

He stands, his brow furrowing for a moment as he sways on his feet.

"Father?" I ask, my heart skipping a beat in my chest as I jump up and hurry over to stand at his elbow.

I press a gentle hand to his side, but he waves me off. Merelda is at his side a second later, taking his weight as she wraps her arm around his waist and levels me with a look.

"See to it that dinner is cleaned up before going to bed, Hazel. I'll tend to your father."

Father meets my gaze, giving me a small nod as if to assure me that he'll be fine. I take a small step away, but can't help linger a moment longer.

"I'm fine, Hazel," he says, reaching out to cup my cheek briefly in the palm of his hand. "Nothing a good night's rest in my own bed won't fix."

Still, I hesitate, watching until the two of them disappear upstairs. Part of me wants to follow after them, to make sure he's really all right, but I don't.

I have to trust that Merelda will take care of him and see to it that he gets the rest he needs. Still, it takes me another moment to force aside the pit of worry in my stomach.

I'd better not get caught standing around, or Merelda will certainly find a way to punish me. Turning, I begin collecting the dishes from the table.

Thankfully, Cyprian and Amadeus have already disappeared, which is a small relief. As I clear the table, wash the dishes, and straighten up the kitchen, my worry only seems to grow. I can't help feeling as if I shouldn't have let Merelda handle things. That I should have insisted on helping take care of Father.

Merelda isn't exactly the most understanding. She may not see to it that he gets the rest he needs.

Hard as I try, I can't push the worry and regret from my mind.

It's not like Father to fall ill, even when traveling ... This thought haunts me as I finally make my way upstairs for the night.

Passing by my father's room, I note the flickering light beneath the door and find myself stopping just outside it. I hesitate for a second, glancing about the dark hall before stepping closer to press my ear to the wooden door.

Frowning, I hear urgent whispering from within. Closing my eyes, I try to focus, holding my breath in an effort to hear better.

"...honestly, Leoric. She is much too old to be this useless," Merelda says, her tone harsh and demanding. "She does little around the house but mope and whine while you are away ... and you should have seen the state I caught her in not moments after you left!"

"I'm sure there must be some sort of misunderstanding—"

Merelda gasps, a strangled sob escaping her.

"How could you question me?" she wails. "Really, Leoric, if I didn't know better, I'd think you didn't care for me at all. You should know how much it pains me to tell you this, but they're my sons. I have to protect them, even if it means from your daughter, the little temptress. I will not allow her to drag our family into such a scandal as that. You should be thanking me for bringing this up before she ruins her own prospects."

My blood turns cold as I listen to her fill my father's ears with lies. For a moment, I'm overcome with disgust and rage. How dare she say such things to him about me! My fists clench as my stomach knots sickeningly.

"She must be wed, immediately. Otherwise, things will only take a turn for the worse. She is a distraction to me and my boys, and I won't allow her to go unchecked for another fortnight."

I push away from the door, breathing hard, before I can do something foolish. More than anything, I want to burst into their room and defend myself, but I know doing so would only cause more trouble.

Still, it takes me longer than I'd like to admit before I can shove the idea from my mind entirely.

Quietly making my way down the hall toward my own room, I make a mental note to speak to Father tomorrow.

First thing, if I can.

He needs to hear what I have to say before she poisons his mind any further toward me.

Confident that I'll be able to sort this mess out in the morning, I close the door to my small, cold room behind me and bar it in place.

Except, by morning, Father is unwell. Too unwell to even make it downstairs to eat.

Merelda is wordless as she hurries about the house, spending most of the morning locked in her private room as strange sounds come from within. It's the first time I've seen her look so worried, and it only adds to my own stress.

Collecting a small plate of food and mug of steaming tea on a tray, I quietly make my way up to Father's bedroom. My nose wrinkles at the horrific scent of steamed herbs that wafts out from beneath the door in heavy waves.

"Where do you think you're going, girl?"

I glance back to find Merelda standing at the top of the stairs, her eyes narrowed on me and hands on her hips.

"I-I just wanted to see him," I answer. "He needs something to eat to keep his strength up."

"No," she says with a shake of her head. "I won't have you fretting about causing him more stress. You'll only make things worse."

"But—"

"Give me that," she orders, stepping toward me to snatch the tray from my hands. "Now, leave him alone to rest."

With that, she sends me off to scrub every inch of the kitchen as well as a half-dozen other chores I'm sure are only meant to keep me out of the house.

At least Amadeus seems to have vanished instead of lurking in the shadows, waiting to pounce and make my day worse. Still, the hours drag on as I tend to every chore Merelda has tossed my way, all the while hoping for some good news upon my return.

Dinner is a quiet affair. Father's chair sits empty, and I find myself unable to tear my eyes away from it.

Dipping my spoon into the chicken bone and vegetable soup I'd spent the afternoon preparing, I barely taste anything past my worry.

Merelda is quiet as she sips her second or third glass of wine, and neither Amadeus or Cyprian say a word, the sound of their knives dragging across the plates filling the air.

"Hazel," my stepmother says, shattering the silence between us, "I'd nearly forgotten the surprise I have for your birthday."

It's only now that I remember that today is my birthday. My spirits sink slightly as I glance back at where Father should be sitting, laughing and smiling with us.

After a moment, I realize that Merelda is impatiently awaiting a reply from me as she clears her throat. Stifling a sigh, I turn my attention back to her.

"What sort of surprise?"

A smile pulls at her lips, making my stomach flip as I warily await her answer.

"It's quite the surprise indeed," she says. "I've finally found a suitable match for you. It's high time, too. Gods know you aren't getting any younger. Any longer, and I was beginning to fear your looks would sour before we could marry you off."

She lets out a bitter laugh at this before the room fills with silence again.

I blink twice, sure that I've misheard her. But, from the way her eyes flash in triumph, I know I haven't.

49

I'm to be married off.

I've always known this day would come. From the moment she first stepped foot in this house, she's been all too eager to see me gone. Now, it appears she'll finally get her way.

The weighty silence is broken by Cyprian pushing his chair away from the table. The wood scraping against the floor, causing me to wince as I glance at him. His eyes flash with anger, his lip curled up in disgust as he stands and storms out of the room.

Unable to stop myself, I let out a snort. Shouldn't I be the one doing the storming out of here?

"Have you nothing to say about this good news?" Merelda asks, as if her youngest son didn't just throw a fit of his own.

I take a moment to collect my thoughts before meeting her gaze.

"What does my father think of this?"

"He's elated, of course," Merelda says, leaning back in her chair as she sips from her glass. "We agreed to it last night. It's something I've been working tirelessly toward, and he was thrilled to know I've finally found you a suitable match."

I stare at her as her smile only seems to grow wider. The timing of all this doesn't sit right with me. Surely, Father would have mentioned something long before now. Even if it was simply to let me know that they were looking.

Now, he's far too ill to confirm that any of this is even true. If this is what he wants for me, what he thinks is best for me, then I won't question their decision ... but I need to hear it from his lips.

Not Merelda's.

"Who?" I ask, though I'm almost too afraid to put a name to my future husband. Afraid that learning it might make this all too real. "Who have you matched me with?"

"Lord Payne."

Merelda's smile is as cold as it is cruel.

I open my mouth to say something, but no words come. Closing my mouth, I swallow past the lump quickly forming in my throat even as her eyes flash in victory.

"When?" I ask, the word barely a squeak.

"You're to be wed as soon as we can reach an agreement on your dowry."

6

HAZEL

I stare at Merelda for a long moment as I try to process everything that she's just told me.

Lord Payne is at least my father's age, if not several years older. I've seen him around town, his eyes always trailing after the young maidens as they go about their days.

If the rumors I've heard are to be even somewhat believed, his behavior behind closed doors would make even the most hardened of men shudder.

And this is the man Merelda and Father mean to marry me to?

"No," I say quietly, startling myself. "I will not marry him."

Amadeus lets out an amused snort at this, suddenly reminding me that he's still sitting with us. I shoot a withering look his way as I shove my chair back.

Unlike Cyprian's dramatic exit, mine is far more awkward as my skirts get caught in the legs of the chair, nearly causing me to trip as I rise to my feet. I'm too slow as I try to make a speedy exit, and Merelda is quicker on her feet.

Blocking my exit, her face twists as she approaches me.

"You will do exactly as I tell you, girl," she hisses, her hand connecting with my cheek before I have a chance to move.

Her eyes flash as she glares down at me, waiting for my reaction. With a stinging cheek, tears flood my eyes, but I refuse to let them fall. I will not give her the satisfaction of knowing the depth of the pain she's caused me.

"You should thank me," Merelda says, straightening. "I could have matched with someone far worse. At least Lord Payne is wealthy enough to care for you ... at least until he grows bored."

"I will *never* thank you for this."

Her eyes narrow on me as I take a step back, putting enough distance between us that I'm confident she won't be able to strike me again so easily. Merelda's nostrils flare as her face colors at my insolence.

I'm not sure what she expected from me upon announcing my upcoming nuptials, but she certainly mustn't have expected me to be happy about them ... let alone thankful.

No, I will not thank her for handing me over to the likes of Lord Payne. The moment Father is well enough to hear me out, I will plead with him not to make me marry this man.

Merelda steps forward, her finger pointed at me as if to drive her point home.

"You should be grateful," she starts, "I could have had you out on the streets, whored out to the first man who'd take you if—"

I can't stand to hear another word of her voice. Of her believing she's finally getting rid of me, as she's been trying to do for the last six years.

The backs of my eyes burning, I send one final glare in her direction before turning and fleeing the dining room.

Tears blur my vision as I make my way through the house and out the back door, unsure of where my feet are taking me. Not that it matters. Wherever I go, she'll find me sooner or later, should she truly want to.

Somehow, I find myself back in Father's ruined workshop.

Except, it's not ruined.

Blinking, I glance around the room. Gone is the destruction from yesterday. The once toppled jars and tins have been righted, the broken glass swept away, and the only evidence of anything having occurred here being the stains too stubborn to be lifted.

Who could have done this, let alone had the time?

I step further into the room, my eye catching on the easel in the back corner.

My painting.

It's been fixed, or at least, someone has tried to fix it. It's far from perfect, but the once-smeared globs of oil paint have been worked into somewhat familiar shapes.

Staring at it, confusion clouds my mind.

Is it possible Father came down here in the middle of

the night? I can't see him having the time, let alone the energy to do so.

Sparing the rest of the workshop another glance, I press my fingers to my temples as my mind swims with the heavy smell of turpentine.

Clearly, I must not be thinking or seeing straight.

I need rest, and tomorrow I'll find a way to speak to Father about this arrangement with Lord Payne and the workshop.

———

The late morning sun filters dustily in through the window at the end of the hall as I pace just outside Father's bedroom.

Merelda has tears in her eyes as she worries her skirts in a chair nearby. We don't speak as we wait to hear what the doctor has to say.

I'd been woken at the crack of dawn to fetch him when Father's breathing had become too labored for her liking. I hate to say it, but I'm thankful for her quick thinking ... even if it meant her dragging me from my sleep and sending me racing off to town in the dark.

The minutes drag on until the door to their bedroom finally opens, and I stop my pacing. The doctor, an older man with dark gray hair and more wrinkles than facial features, steps out into the hall.

His face is grim as he takes Merelda and me in, quietly shutting the door behind him. He doesn't say anything for a long moment as I shift uncomfortably on my feet.

Each passing second of quiet has worry clenching its cruel fingers harder and harder around my heart, until I'm almost certain that I won't be able to survive whatever news he has to tell us.

Surely, if it were good news, he would've spat it out already. And yet, I cannot help but hope.

"Well?" Merelda finally asks in annoyance, rising from her chair. "Out with it already."

The old man clears his throat a few times, obviously flustered.

"I-I'm afraid I'm not entirely sure what's wrong with him," he says. "His breathing has only grown more strained in the last hour. I've tried everything that I can think on him, but nothing seems to be working. I ... I'm afraid he's come down with something that even I have no medicine for."

Merelda lets out a snort of disgust.

"Fine, then I'll just call for the doctor from the next town over, perhaps *he'll* actually be of some use to me and my husband."

I watch the doctor bristle at Merelda's empty threat. Especially when I grew up hearing how much of a bumbling fool the doctor in the next town over is.

"That won't be necessary," the doctor continues. "You'll only end up wasting more time and money. There's no remedy for whatever he has. No matter how many doctors you call in, they will all say the same."

Tears sting my eyes as I try to process what he's just said. If it's something he can't treat, then how is father supposed to get better?

"Which is?" Merelda presses, giving voice to my own thoughts.

The doctor runs a hand over his tired face, letting out a small sigh.

"If he is lucky, then he has a month left, perhaps two, in the best of cases ... but it's unlikely he will ever be lucid again."

"No," I gasp, taking a stumbling step backward.

Merelda shoots me a hard look as she steps closer to the doctor ushering him back into the bedroom. Their voices fall quiet as the door closes behind them, but it doesn't matter. I've stopped listening.

I can't imagine a world that doesn't involve my father always being here. It's impossible.

The doctor must be wrong.

How is it possible that Father has only been given months to live? He was perfectly healthy just the other day. Before he set off on his last journey, nothing seemed amiss.

Pressing a hand to my stomach, I turn away from the door.

No, I can't lose him. I won't allow it. He's all I have left.

Without him, I'll be alone in this world with nothing but a cold stepmother hell bent on selling me off to a monster of a man.

My heart clenches at the thought of a world without my father. Did I not lose enough already when Mother was taken from us? Must I now suffer his loss as well?

It feels as though my whole world is crumbling around me, the stones of a once happy life now threatening to crush me beneath them until I'm nothing more than dust. I almost welcome the thought as I step from the house and into the gardens.

I wipe uselessly at the tears that spill over my cheeks as I walk. Merelda will not hesitate to cast me out, married or not, the moment Father takes his last breath.

That is a future not many could survive. Without anywhere to go or any coin to my name, I'd be far worse off than I am now.

I'd almost certainly have no choice but to allow her to marry me off. To sell me to the pig that is Lord Payne.

A shiver runs down my spine at the thought, and I shake my head.

No, I mustn't think like this, not yet. For all I know, the doctor could be wrong. Father could still pull through and smile upon me once again.

Even the doctor couldn't say exactly what was wrong with him. Perhaps there's still a chance.

A fresh wave of tears fall as I realize how much I still have to tell Father. I've wasted too much time upset about the future and worried about the present. I didn't stop to tell him how much I love and adore him.

Now, I may never get the chance.

Choking on a sob, I head further away from the house before Merelda can come to find me. I'm not prepared to deal with her cruelty in a moment like this.

Racing down the hill, I make my way through our bit of forest and field and into the apple orchard that belongs to our neighbors. At the far end of which is a small grove of overgrown trees, the perfect place to disappear into, as I have many times in the past. Among them, a giant elm that has always kindly offered me refuge from Merelda and her sons.

Reaching the elm, I press the palm of my hand to the bark. Inhaling deeply, I try my best to ground myself as I calm my racing heart and endless tears.

Here, I am safe from all that is wrong in the world ... or so I try to tell myself as I tilt my head back to look up into the leaf-framed sky.

Except, it's a boot that enters my vision instead.

Stumbling away from the tree, I realize too late that my secret spot isn't empty. Someone is already here.

Looking up, I meet Cyprian's gaze. He blinks back at me in surprise before dropping from the branch he's perched himself on.

Of course, he *would* be here. Spinning on my heel, I hurry to get away from this place. Away from him, but he catches my wrist.

"Hazel," he says, his voice low and soft. "Wait."

"Let me go."

He reaches for my face, turning it slowly toward him so that I have no choice but to meet his eyes. I tense, half expecting Amadeus to step out of a nearby bush to commend his brother on once again cornering me.

It dawns on me that with Father dying, there will no longer be anyone to protect me from them.

"I'm so sorry, Hazel," Cyprian says, his eyes searching my face. "I-I'm sorry for what my mother has done, what she plans to do to you ... but worse still, my heart breaks to hear the news about your father."

My mouth falls open in surprise, unable to form words

in response to this. I don't know what I expected him to say, but it wasn't this.

"I know what it feels like," he continues, his voice rough, "to watch the man who raised you, who taught you everything, who loved you at your worst ... to watch him lie there, dying. I know what it feels like to be utterly helpless, unable to stop what's happening."

His words wash over me, painful and yet somehow comforting to hear. I let out a small whimper, and a new wave of tears overtakes me. The next thing I know, I'm a sobbing mess as he pulls me into his arms.

Cyprian's touch is gentle, almost tender as he wipes away my tears. I stiffen for a moment at his touch, but then I tuck my face into his chest and let my heartache out.

There's no pretending at this point, anyway.

I don't know how long I let him hold me as I cry, but by the time my tears finally dry, his shirt is wet beneath me.

Suddenly, I'm all too aware that it's Cyprian who holds me to his chest. That it's my stepbrother who's cradling me in his arms as my heart shatters to pieces.

I pull back nearly as quickly as I'm able to process this, my eyes shifting away from him. Unable to glance at him as I feel my cheeks burn with shame, I do my best to try to pull myself together.

I never should have let him see me this vulnerable. Any moment now, I'm sure he'll find a way to use it against me.

"I should go," I say after a moment, my voice watery and broken.

"No," he replies, taking me aback, "I have a better idea."

My heart skips a beat in my chest as I glance up at him,

and he offers me a smile. A genuine smile that's soft and full of promise. A smile I've never seen on him before.

Then, my eyes shift to his outstretched hand, and I realize he intends to lead me somewhere.

Part of me knows I shouldn't go anywhere with him ... that doing so wouldn't be wise, and yet, I find my hand slipping into his.

Without another word, he turns and pulls me away from the grove of trees. Hand in hand we walk through the orchard, over the broken fence, and away from home.

I'm curious where he intends to bring me, but I don't give voice to the question. Silence wraps around us like a heavy cloak as we step out onto the dusty road and toward town.

7

HAZEL

Sitting at a table in the back of a smoky tavern, I take another sip from the goblet in my hand.

It's my first time tasting wine, and I'm surprised by the pleasant berry-like sweetness of it.

Unlike Cyprian, who has ordered round after round of his own ale, I'm slow to finish my first glass.

Around us, townsfolk come and go as they order drinks and food, chatting to one another and occasionally nodding to us.

"When I was six, he took me out to the woodshed," Cyprian tells me, drawing my attention back to him, a fond smile on his face. "He handed me an axe that was nearly half my size and taught me how to chop wood. Of course, later, Mother gave him an earful for allowing me to do servant's work and getting my hands calloused from the rough wood."

"I don't think I've ever seen Amadeus so much as glance at an axe."

62

Cyprian laughs, shaking his head.

"I doubt he's ever touched one either. He'd probably break his dainty little fingers if he tried. "

I have to stifle a snort at this, coughing as a bit of wine catches in my throat. Cyprian pats me on the back before we share a laugh together.

I don't know how long we've been here, the drawn windows letting little outside light in, but I've enjoyed getting to know Cyprian as we've shared stories of our fathers and the happier days of our childhoods.

I was wary at first when he led me here, and then again when he handed me the goblet of wine that's long since gone warm in my hands. But now, listening to him talk and watching the way his eyes soften as he looks at me, I almost feel relaxed.

My gaze slips past Cyprian as a middle-aged couple approach the table, and I straighten in my seat, wary of them as their eyes land on me. Vaguely, as if pulled through a hazy wall of memories, I realize I recognize the man. A merchant, he'd once commissioned an illustrated book of fairytales for his wife for the birth of their firstborn child.

"Excuse us for interrupting," the man says nervously, worrying the rings on his hand. "We've just heard the news of your father falling ill. He's a fine man, a good man, if ever there was one. We just wanted to let you know that we're all praying that death won't steal him away from us just yet."

At my side, Cyprian goes still at this, his fingers whitening around his mug. Carefully, I set my own goblet down, unsure of how best to respond to them.

Father was, is, a well-respected and loved man in our

town, in most towns, in fact. Nearly everyone here has some book or work in their possession that came from him. As much as it pains me to be reminded of it, it warms my heart to see my own grief reflected back in this man's face.

"Thank you," I finally manage.

With a nod, the couple leave.

Silence stretches between Cyprian and me. I watch as he downs the rest of his current ale before glancing at me. The pain I see in his eyes is almost too much to bear.

"They're right, you know."

"What?"

"About your father," he clarifies. "He's a good man. Far better than I or my family deserve."

"Oh."

I'm not sure what else to say to this, having thought this very thing myself many times over the years. Instead, I take another sip of my wine.

"In some ways, your father has been more of a parent to me than my own was," Cyprian says as I continue to drink from my goblet, my thoughts growing hazier. "I'd heard whispers that there was a man in town who dealt in tricks and magic, and I was desperate to see it for myself. Of course, my mother refused to go into the city, and my father had already left on business for the day. So, naturally, I decided to go by myself."

"Just to see a street performer?" I ask.

"I know it sounds ridiculous, but I didn't know that's what they meant at the time," he answers. "Mind you, I was just seven. Slipping from the house was easy, I've always had a knack for it, but as I wandered further and further into the city, I suddenly realized I had no idea where to go … let alone how to get home. I stood, overwhelmed, in the city square crying for help as people bustled by without so much as a glance my way."

I reach out to place a comforting hand on Cyprian's arm at this, my own heart breaking for the lost little boy.

"I thought I'd be lost forever, until one man stopped," he continues, his thumb running absentmindedly over the handle of his mug. "He had kind eyes and colorful, ink-stained fingertips. I remember thinking he was some kind of magical being. In many ways, he was. Crouching so that we could see eye to eye, he asked me why I was crying. I told him I was lost and couldn't find my way back home."

"You must have been terrified."

"I was, and thinking back on it now, I was lucky I wasn't kidnapped," Cyprian admits. "I could tell he was busy on his own business, his arms full of parcels, but still, without a second thought he dropped what he was doing to help me. He bought me lunch and held my hand tight in his own. It took all day before I finally recognized the way home. When my mother answered the front door, she hadn't even realized I was gone."

"Oh," I breathe, knowing all too well the feeling.

"Of course, she acted the part of a bereaved mother the second she was told what happened. My own father was still away on business, but she insisted he come in and have some of her special tea, despite him trying to refuse. As my mother was preparing the tea, he asked me if I liked books. I shook my head, and he told me that was about to change. I still remember the sparkle in his eyes as he reached into his jacket pocket and pulled out a small parcel tied neatly with a red ribbon."

I blink as it suddenly dawns on me that Cyprian is talking about Father, my father.

"What happened next?" I ask, my focus on his story sharpening despite the dull hum in my head.

"He gave it to me, and inside was the most beautifully illustrated children's book. I couldn't read yet, but I didn't have to. The pictures spoke more than any words could."

Cyprian clears his throat, shifting on the bench to reach into his pants pocket before gently placing a tiny, worn book down on the table between us.

"You kept it, all this time?" I gasp, reaching out to gently trace the beautiful lines that have now become worn and faded over the years.

"Of course, I kept it," he answers softly, his eyes distant. "Your father showed me more kindness in one day than I'd known my whole life."

A smile tugs at the corners of my lips, despite the ache in my heart. I'm not surprised to hear such a sweet story about my father, his kind soul never would have allowed him to leave a child crying alone in the streets.

"There's something else," Cyprian says, making me glance up into his sad eyes. "Look."

He opens the small book on the table to the first page. There's a beautiful illustration of a little brown-haired and blue-eyed girl holding a chicken ... and below it an inscription.

To my darling, Hazel. I wish you the happiest of birthdays, with all the love this world has to offer.

I stare at it, barely able to comprehend what I'm seeing.

"I-I don't understand. I've never seen this book in my life."

"I think he gave me what was supposed to be your birthday gift," Cyprian says, his jaw working for a moment as if the words are difficult for him. "I think he couldn't bear for a child not to have a love for books."

"That does sound like him," I say quietly, my fingers gently tracing the lines of my name.

"I know it sounds stupid, but this book changed my life. Your father changed my life, Hazel ... and—"

"Oh gods," a ruddy-faced woman interrupts, dropping onto the bench across from us. "Is he dead?"

"What?" I blink in shock at her as Cyprian slips the tiny book safely back into his pocket.

"Your father, is he dead?"

"I-I don't think so," I answer, my stomach twisting sickeningly at the thought.

"Oh, thank the gods," she sighs, practically flattening herself against the table in relief. "I was worried you being here meant ... Well, you know."

The woman rambles on, jumping from topic to topic so abruptly that I can hardly keep up. My fingers tighten around my own goblet as I listen to her tell story after story of my father and how terribly sorry that she is that he is unwell.

"Have you finished your drink?" Cyprian asks when the woman is finally dragged away from us by her need to relieve herself.

Glancing down at my goblet, I'm surprised to find it empty.

"Yes," I answer with a nod.

"Good, let me get you another. If I'd realized you'd be accosted by nearly ever patron here, I'd have brought you somewhere quieter."

"I don't mind the noise," I say. "It keeps my own thoughts at bay."

"Very well, I'll be back in just a moment," he says.

The way my head is already spinning, perhaps I shouldn't allow him to fetch me a second goblet, but I don't stop him as he crosses the room. I watch as he leans against the bar on the far side of the tavern, chatting familiarly with the bartender.

Until something catches my attention out of the corner of my eye.

At first, I think it's a trick of the light, or perhaps my mind ... but I could almost swear that I saw something like a giant inky shadow slip into the tavern.

A shiver runs down my spine as I peer closer at the back corner of the room. Slowly, the shadows seem to swirl and pull together, almost as if they're trying to reshape themselves into the form of an enormous horned creature.

My eyes widen, my heart pounding in my chest as I open my mouth to say something.

"There you are, Hazel," a voice says, startling me as I glance away from the shadows to find a woman standing next to the table. "I was beginning to worry I wouldn't find you in time."

"I'm sorry, do I know you?" I ask, my eyes flickering back

68

to the corner to find it completely empty of any shadow monsters.

"Not yet," she answers. "Just know, should you ever need help, my child, you need only come looking for it."

Our eyes meet, hers a golden hue that seems altogether wrong. It must be the glow from the fire across the tavern, or perhaps it's the wine playing more tricks on me. I thought I was fine, but it's becoming clearer by the second that I'm not.

"What do you mean?"

"You'll know when the time comes. Listen to your heart, for the mind can often play tricks."

Blinking at her, I open my mouth to ask her to clarify what she's just said, just as Cyprian reappears. Our drinks in hand, he scowls at the tiny woman as he stares down at her.

"Be gone with you, witch," he growls, placing a new goblet-full of wine before me.

The woman says nothing, simply wrapping her dark cloak tighter around her before giving me one last look and disappearing into the crowd.

I frown as I try to watch her go. There was a seriousness to her words that seemed to stab me right through my heart. As though she was trying to tell me something important without outright saying it.

Not that any of it made any sense to me. Not that anything makes any sense to me right now.

I turn my attention back to the wine before me, hesitating for a second before raising it to my lips.

The sweetness of the wine has grown more sour with time, as has my stomach.

As the day passes, more and more people begin to spill into the tavern. Many stop to chat with Cyprian, and it's impossible to miss the disapproving looks and raised eyebrows that are being directed at me.

Even as I hide my face in my goblet, making much quicker work of my second helping of wine. Standing, Cyprian takes my now-empty cup and makes his way back to the bar for more, my eyes trailing after him as he goes.

I don't know why I never noticed how much his presence fills a room. Here, he almost seems to command attention as people quickly move out of his way.

"Here," Cyprian says upon his return, handing me a mug this time.

"I don't think I can drink anymore," I say, the words thick on my tongue.

"It's just wat—"

We're suddenly interrupted as a large man bumps into the table, knocking Cyprian's elbow as he leans drunkenly over it, causing some of the water to splash on me.

"Cyprian, my boy," the man bellows, laughing as he reaches a sweaty arm around my stepbrother's shoulders, ale sloshing out of his cup. "Now that your newest stepfather is dying, perhaps you'll finally let us have a go at that girl of his. She'd be an orphan then, no reason for you to worry about her reputati—"

I see the thunder on Cyprian's face long before the man has a chance to react. The man's face ripples with the force of Cyprian's fist, spittle and blood flying out as he's thrown off balance and stumbles drunkenly backwards.

"You fucking cu—"

Cyprian is on him before another word can leave the man's mouth.

I'm too shocked to move, watching in horrified awe as Cyprian holds the man up by a handful of his shirt, his other fist pummeling into the man with terrible force. Sweat beads on my stepbrother's forehead, his dark hair forming into clumps as his knuckles bloody and the veins surface along his bare forearms.

The whole tavern is in an uproar now, men scrambling to pull him off the now unconscious stranger, just as I'm distracted by the door opening and a chilly breeze whipping through the room.

Outside, the sky has darkened to a soft purple, and my mind suddenly quiets despite the raucousness around me.

Oh, no ... we've been gone nearly the whole day.

Panic tightens around my chest as I realize what I've done. I'll certainly be punished for this. Merelda will be all too eager for any distraction to keep her mind off Father, of that, I'm sure.

I need to go home now, before I make things any worse for myself.

Standing, the room sways around me.

The wine hits me in full force as I start to tilt, my movements too slow as I reach for the table to stabilize myself and miss.

But I don't fall. Cyprian is there just as suddenly, catching me with an arm around my waist. He pulls me flat against his side as the room fights to right itself. I lean into him, thankful for his strength as he guides me through the crowd toward the door.

People glance at me, and I see their mouths moving but hear nothing but the beating of my heart in my ears. I'm sure it's more kind words about my father.

At least, I hope it is and not them judging me over my current state.

My cheeks burn as I realize how disappointed Father would be if he could see me right now.

"Hazel?" Cyprian asks, concern clear in his voice as my head lulls against his chest.

"Home," I mumble. "I need to go home."

His hands tighten around me as he leads me through the tavern. I hear the man he knocked out just minutes before slur something toward us, but Cyprian doesn't react. Instead, his attention remains fixed on helping me navigate the swaying people as they dive deeper into their cups.

Closing my eyes, I pray that the fog that's settled about me will lift by the time we reach the house.

I'm not sure I want to know what my punishment will be for returning tipsy. Merelda will certainly see to it that I never do this again, that much I know.

Outside the tavern, the evening is once again surprisingly cool. A breeze whips around us, carrying the scent of smoke and rain.

Leaning against Cyprian, he takes my weight as we make our way through town. My thanks to him for helping me right now is stuck on my tongue.

It feels strange to depend on him, to be so vulnerable at his side and not feel as wary as I once did.

Maybe it's the alcohol, or maybe I've truly misjudged him all these years because of the torment his mother and brother have caused me.

Turning, I squint up at him, trying to determine which it is.

He glances down at me, giving me a small reassuring smile.

"You're going to be okay," he says, misreading the look on my face.

The silence stretches between us as we reach the edge of town and begin the trek home along a small winding path through the woods.

I'm surprised by how comfortable I find this moment. How safe I feel even as we move further and further away from town.

With each step, I feel my head clearing as the world begins to right itself again. And yet, I don't immediately step away from his side.

"Well, well, well ... what do we have here?"

My heart drops into my stomach as I glance away from Cyprian to find Amadeus leaning against a tree at the foot of the hill leading to our home. He smirks at us, and I hate the way his eyes flash as they rake over me.

Suddenly, I wish I'd insisted upon standing upright myself. Like this, it must be as clear as day to him that I'm not myself.

"It looks like the gods have finally answered my prayers," Amadeus says, pushing away from the tree to stalk closer. "She drunk, all thanks to you, brother, and it's high time I finally take what's mine."

"No. You're not to lay a finger on her. Do I make myself clear?"

Cyprian shifts slightly so that I'm half-hidden from his brother. This only causes Amadeus' smirk to widen as he takes us in.

Belatedly, I realize Cyprian has just raised the stakes and made taking me all that more immediate and important to his brother ... especially after what happened back in Father's workshop.

My blood runs cold at this thought.

"It's cute, brother," Amadeus says lazily, his eyes narrowing on us. "Don't think for a moment that I can't see what you're doing. Playing protector, finding ways to lower her guard until you can strike. It needn't be so complicated. Let me have her, and I'll make sure you get your chance with her when I'm through."

"Go home, Amadeus," Cyprian growls.

"I don't think I will. In fact, I think I'd rather take her right here, up against this tree. What do you think, brother? Care to stay and watch?"

Without meaning to, I take a step back from Cyprian, and to my surprise, he lets me. A second later, I realize why as he lunges at his brother.

Amadeus stumbles backward as Cyprian lands a hit to his nose. My stomach knots at the crunch of cartilage, and a low curse escapes Amadeus as he presses his palm to his face.

Pulling his hand away, I let out a small gasp. Even with

74

the fading light, it's hard to miss the blood as it drips from his now crooked nose

"You'll pay for that," Amadeus shouts, launching himself toward Cyprian as he easily dodges the attack.

I watch as they throw themselves at each other, frozen in place as a sensation of utter helplessness settles in my stomach. I know I should run. I should get as far away from them as possible, but I can't get my legs to move.

At one point, Amadeus suddenly side steps, turning on me as Cyprian stumbles.

"Hazel, run," Cyprian shouts, glancing at me and giving Amadeus all the distraction he needs.

I gasp in shock as Amadeus whirls on him, landing a hard hit to Cyprian's stomach, causing him to double over as he collapses to his knees with a groan.

Before I can react, Amadeus' hand has wrapped around my wrist. He yanks me to one side, the world spinning around me once again from the sudden movements.

Shoving me back against the rough bark of the tree, Amadeus pins me against it. Sneering down at me, blood coats his lips and chin, adding an extra layer of monstrosity to him as his eyes flash with lust and hatred.

Grabbing me by my throat, he forces my head back before crushing his blood-wet lips to mine. The scent of iron and salt mix as I struggle to push him away, my own lips pressed tightly shut against his onslaught.

He pulls back, his breathing heavy as his fingers tighten around my throat and I gasp for air.

"You will give in to me, even if it's the last thing you do."

Suddenly, Amadeus' eyes widen as he's thrown back

from me. I clutch at my throat just as Cyprian grabs my wrist and begins pulling me up the hill toward the house.

I don't fight him, even as his fingers dig into my wrist. I don't doubt there will be a bruise from his grip in the morning, but that's the least of my concerns right now.

"Stop!" Amadeus screams at us, scrambling to get to his feet.

"Don't look back," Cyprian orders, quickening his pace as I fight to stay on my own two feet.

"Mother will hear of this! Be sure that she'll deal with you both!"

With Amadeus hurrying behind us, we're a garish sight as we make our way up the hill and into our front garden.

My heart leaps into my throat as I see Merelda standing in the door, hands on her hips, as she takes us in.

"What in the seven hells is the meaning of this?" she hisses. "I've been looking everywhere for you, girl."

The hatred in her face is momentarily broken as her eyes shift to her eldest son and the blood smeared across his face.

"My darling boy, what has this whore done to you?!" she gasps, tears shining in her eyes as she hurries over to him.

"I'm fine, Mother," Amadeus tells her before letting out a yelp of pain as he wipes the sleeve of his shirt across his mouth.

"Go, wash the blood from your face. I'll be in to tend to you in a moment."

"Mother—" Cyprian starts, but she holds up a hand to silence him.

"Not a word from you," she snaps. "Nothing, is that understood?"

"But Hazel—"

"I said nothing!" Merelda shrieks. "Another word from your lips, and I'll tan the girl's hide to within an inch of her life."

Cyprian's fingers tighten around my wrist, but he presses his lips into a thin line, the sharp angle of his jaw hardening. Stepping forward, Merelda tugs me from Cyprian's grip, even as he tries to reach for me again.

I give Cyprian a look that stops him in his tracks as Merelda drags me into the house and back to the kitchen. As much as I appreciate what he's done for me, he'll only make things worse trying to help.

Merelda says nothing, but I can feel her anger rolling off in heavy waves, threatening to drown me at any moment.

"I'm at my wit's end with you, girl," she finally says through gritted teeth.

We've come to a stop before two large buckets full of water. Steam curls thickly into the air from one as she kicks out the back of my knees, forcing me to the floor before them.

Before I have a chance to react, Merelda grabs a handful of hair at the back of my head and forces my head down into the steaming water.

It burns, stinging my eyes and filling my nose. I let out a gasp of surprise, the air bubbles that stream out tickling my face as I inhale water out of pure shock.

Just when I'm sure I'm going to drown myself, she pulls

me out. I cough and splutter, gasping for air and just barely managing to get some before she dunks my head into the second bucket.

Ice cold water sends pain rippling through my mind and body. My lungs burn with water as I close my eyes against it, and I can't help wondering if this is how I'm going to die.

Just before the burn becomes too intense to bear any longer, I'm pulled back up for air. Once more, I gulp at the air, fighting my lungs as they try to clear themselves of water first. I don't know how long she intends to punish me like this, or if she means to drown me.

Part of me hopes she does. That she'll end me before I'm forced to live here without my father. Before I'm forced to marry such a vile man as Lord Payne.

Merelda dunks me into both buckets twice more, each time feeling longer than the last. My body goes limp as I give up fighting her, saving what remains of my energy for the brief moments when I surface for air.

I barely manage to catch myself as I'm unexpectedly tossed aside, landing hard on the cold stone floor of the kitchen, gasping and half-drowned. Merelda kicks the toe of her boot roughly into my side, but I can barely let out a whimper despite the pain.

"I expect dinner to be ready in an hour," my stepmother says, glaring down at me as I look up at her. "Don't be late, or there'll be more than this for you to deal with before the night's through."

With a final look of disgust, she turns on her heel and

leaves the kitchen. The door slammed shut behind her, I curl in on myself as my lungs struggle to return to normal.

For a long moment, I don't move as I rest my head against the floor.

As terrible as that was, I'm almost surprised she didn't do worse. Despite my soaked dress, and the bruise that may form where she kicked me, there are no other visible marks of her cruelty.

Not this time.

Somehow, this realization has the hairs at the nape of my neck standing on end.

8

HAZEL

S tanding in the corner of the dining room, I watch as Merelda and her two sons eat. Well, at least Amadeus does. Cyprian does little but push the food around his plate.

When I began to set the table, Merelda had made it clear to me that I would have to wait to eat, as she wasn't in the habit of allowing animals at the table. She'd delivered this news to me with a cold smile, and I had made no argument against it.

I'd decided it was better than having to endure eating with them. A cold dinner was little punishment in comparison.

"The peas are rubbery," Amadeus complains.

"You won't have to deal with the girl's cooking for much longer, dear," Merelda says. "It's honestly a miracle we've yet to die from her lack of skill. Shame to think her mother was such a great cook."

"And a beauty, too."

80

"Shame she inherited little from either of her parents," Merelda says with a sigh. "I suppose not every child can be so lucky."

The two share a look, content with speaking about me as though I'm not standing but a few feet away from them. I press my lips together, doing my best to ignore their comments as my eyes slip to Cyprian.

He doesn't say a word, his eyes focused down on his plate, his shoulders tense. If I didn't know better, I'd almost think he'd been punished just as I had.

Suddenly, Merelda's attention shifts to her youngest son.

"I'd almost forgotten you were here, Cyprian," she says, reaching for her wine glass, a slow smile pulling at her lips.

I've seen her look at me this way, and it never ends well.

For some reason, I feel the urge to give Cyprian some kind of warning. Not that he's so much as glanced in my direction since he arrived in the dining room just minutes after his mother and brother were seated.

Though, he's probably been ignoring me in front of them for my own good.

"Come now," Merelda continues, pausing to take a sip of her wine, "don't look so sullen. I have good news for you."

"Somehow, I doubt that," Cyprian mumbles, his voice hard.

Merelda's smile slips slightly, but she presses on none-theless, "I've finally found a suitable wife for you."

Silence fills the room.

Cyprian stiffens, his hand stilling as he stops pushing the peas around his plate. Then, too slowly, he sets it down.

Lifting his eyes to meet Merelda's, I can't quite see what passes between them, but I watch as the smile falls from her face.

"No."

The word slips softly from his lips, his voice altogether terrifying in its calmness.

"I'm afraid it's not up for discussion, dear," Merelda continues, her own eyes suddenly unable or unwilling to meet his. "It's high time that you were settled with a family of your own. Perhaps then you'll finally manage to stay out of the tavern long enough to think straight."

"I have no interest in marriage."

Merelda clicks her tongue at this.

"Really, Cyprian, I'm not sure where I went wrong with you. You should be more worried about strengthening the family name. It's in our best interest to have you producing heirs as soon as possible. Preferably within the next year."

"I would much rather sire a thousand bastard children than marry a woman you chose for me," Cyprian snarls.

"Don't be such a fool," Merelda snaps.

Shoving his chair back from the table, it topples over as he stands and glares down at his mother.

"And what of Amadeus? He's the eldest, shouldn't siring an heir be of his concern, not mine?"

"Of course, but you of all people should know that your brother is special. He can't just be married off to any wench of decent breeding," Merelda responds without hesitation. "He needs someone nearly as special as he is. Someone I have yet to find."

"I'll never be wed, Mother," Cyprian says, the heaviness

of his voice sending goosebumps racing across my skin, "let alone to some wench, as you so delicately put it, that you've chosen. I'd rather our family name die with me than give you such pleasure."

I let out a small gasp at this before quickly clamping a hand over my mouth, but it's too late. I've already drawn everyone's attention to my presence. Their expressions are nearly as surprised as my own, as if for one moment, I was truly forgotten in the shadows of the room.

Merelda's cold eyes flash to me, anger in them as she takes me in.

"Amadeus and Cyprian, leave us this instant."

Amadeus is quick to obey, the cruel grin he shoots my way all too familiar. Cyprian, however hesitates as he glances over at me, his expression searching, questioning. I give him the smallest of nods, and he turns to follow his brother from the room.

A tense moment passes in their wake as I wait for what's to come.

"Do not think for an instant that I've so easily forgotten about you, girl," she hisses. "I'll have you wed before you can poison my son against me any further. Is that understood?"

Her reminder of my imminent betrothal to Lord Payne is unnecessary as I've barely had a chance to forget. Not wanting to provoke her further, I nod once.

Moving to clear the dishes, Merelda stands and steps into my path, giving me no choice but to glance up at her. I hate the way victory seems to have settled into her features.

"In fact," she says, "Lord Payne will be arriving within

the hour. Apparently, he'd like to ... take a look at his future wife before coming to an agreement on your worth. Speaking of, we must see what we can do about your appearance."

With that, she reaches out to grab me. I wince as her fingers dig into the hollows of my shoulders. If only it were the first time that she's held me in place in such a manner.

Her eyes move over my body as she takes me in. With a disappointed sigh, she shakes her head.

"Heaven help me, I'm not sure there's enough time in the day to make you presentable, girl."

Clicking her tongue at me, she grabs my wrist, dragging me out of the dining room. For a moment, I consider fighting her, but I think better of it as she pulls me toward her small private room and curiosity gets the better of me.

I'd only ever been inside once, and only then for a second before Merelda had found me and dragged me out screaming by a handful of my hair. That had been nearly six years ago now.

Opening the door, she pushes me inside before stepping in and slamming the door shut behind us.

The room is nothing like what I remember. Where shelves upon shelves of strange herbs and mixtures had once been, they now stood empty save for a pitcher, a piece of cloth, a few small jars, and a silver comb.

In the center of the room is a wooden tub, half-filled with water. A small chest is tucked away in the far corner of the room, and beside it an empty chair.

With a heavy sigh, Merelda steps past me to drag the

chair closer to the tub. Her eyes lift to me, and with yet another sigh, she shakes her head.

I can't help but frown as I glance down at myself, taking in the simple dress and my limp braid. I'd never worried about my looks before, they'd been the least of my concerns over the years ... but now, I almost hope that my father was lying when he'd called me beautiful.

Perhaps, if I'm lucky and the gods can find it in their hearts to pity me, Lord Payne will find me wanting.

"Sit," Merelda orders, turning to grab the pitcher and washcloth off the shelves.

I move to do as I'm told without a second thought, not wanting to invite any more of her anger toward me. Turning back to me, she scowls.

"Don't be so daft, girl," she huffs. "Undress and get into the tub. The chair is for me."

My cheeks burn with heat at the thought of disrobing in front of her. I open my mouth to argue, to beg her to let me wash myself, but then I decide better of it.

Surely, begging would only make things worse.

Rising slowly to my feet, I work the tight knot of my apron before moving on to the lacing of my dress. Far too soon, I'm letting both fall to my feet in soft pools of old fabric.

I start to step into the tub, but Merelda stops me, grabbing my arm to turn me toward her. Her eyes rake over my body, and I want nothing more than to cross my arms over my chest to hide myself from her ruthless gaze.

She circles me, appraising me like a piece of livestock before finally gesturing toward the bath. Reaching out, she cups each of my breasts in her hand, as if weighing their worth.

"Small, but they'll have to do. Get in. Thank the heavens I had the good sense to have a new dress made for you," she says. "At least it'll help make up for some of what you lack in feminine beauty, if only through distraction."

I step into the tub, a shiver instantly racing across my skin.

"It's cold."

"Good, it'll bring out a healthy flush in your skin. Now, sit!"

I lower myself into the water, trying to allow my body a chance to adjust, but I'm not given the chance.

Merelda leans over to dip the pitcher into the water before pouring icy water over my head. I barely have a chance to gasp in shock before she's wet the washcloth and slapped it against my skin, causing me to flinch.

Her cold laugh fills the room as she attacks my skin, and I have to brace myself against the edge of the tub. I flinch under the roughness of her hands.

The way she scrubs at my hair and skin, I worry that I'll be covered in bruises by the time she's through, if not rubbed entirely bald and raw. There's not a single thing gentle about the way she touches me, though I'd be a fool to expect otherwise.

"Stand," Merelda orders, rising from her chair, once she's satisfied that my hair and back are thoroughly cleansed.

Shivering as I get to my feet, the cold water drips from the long lengths of my hair and down my curves. Merelda frowns at my naked form, and I try my best to calm my shaking body, but it's impossible.

Re-wetting the cloth, she continues to wash the rest of me, paying extra attention to my breasts even as I grimace in pain at the roughness of the cloth. Finally, she steps back, seemingly satisfied that she's scrubbed away every speck of dirt from my skin.

"Now, sit," she says, this time pointing at the chair, "while I figure out what to do with that unruly hair of yours."

Muttering about the wretched darkness of the thick waves that cascade down my back, Merelda reaches for the silver comb.

"It's truly a shame that you look so much like your mother," Merelda tells me as she yanks the comb through my hair, tugging hard enough on a tangle to bring tears to my eyes. "All the bad with none of the good, that is."

Biting my tongue, I force myself to remain silent. If I were to say what I'm thinking, it would only cause me more pain at her hand.

It sickens me to see how cooperative I've become, but then I realize what's made me this way.

Fear.

Fear has taught me to be obedient, and I shudder in shame at the thought. Father would hate to see how docile I've become, if only in an effort to keep the peace.

He'd always taught me to be bold, and yet, Merelda had found a way to break me.

"How is my father?" I ask, unable to stop myself.

My stepmother's hands falter for a moment before she

steps away to set down the comb. She doesn't answer my question, instead busying herself with my hair again.

Her fingers are rough against my scalp as she twists and braids half my hair up, leaving some free to flow down over my back and shoulders.

"Get up," Merelda orders, and I do my best to ignore the chill that's working its way into my bones as she crosses the room to unlock the small chest.

Returning to me, she shoves a simple chemise and dress into my hands, and I stare down at them. The dress is a deep brown color that will only make my skin look all the paler, but perhaps that's the entire point.

Pulling the chemise over my head and then the dress, I note the deepness of the neckline as Merelda moves to lace up the back of the dress. I gasp as she pulls the laces tight, forcing my body to conform to the shape of the dress with each tug.

Turning me around, I catch a glimpse of myself in a small looking glass hanging by the door. The dress hugs my body, giving me curves that I didn't realize I had, the swell of my breasts nearly spilling entirely from the wide, open neckline. My heartbeat quickens as I realize how little of my form has been left to the imagination.

One wrong move, and I'll be put entirely on display.

"Stand tall, girl," Merelda snaps. "I won't have anyone thinking I put up with a gremlin in this house."

I straighten my shoulders as best I can, forcing my eyes away from my reflection as Merelda circles me again. Her frown deepens for a moment before she steps forward and pinches my cheeks, hard.

My yelp of surprise seems to satisfy her as she brushes her hands over her skirts.

"That'll have to do," she says with a disappointed sigh. "If only you were prettier, bigger bosomed, even ... but this will have to do. Let's just hope his sight isn't what it used to be."

Glancing around the room, she suddenly grows flustered as she mutters a curse under her breath.

"Come, quickly now," she barks, grabbing me by the wrist as she hurries us from her private room and up the stairs. "Wait here, don't you dare move a muscle, do you hear me?"

"Yes."

She eyes me for a long moment, before slipping into my father's room. It's too dark to see anything inside before she closes the door behind her, a strange aroma wafting out around me.

I frown, unable to place the scent, though there's something familiar about it that prickles the back of my mind. Before I have a chance to think of it, Merelda returns, a golden bottle in hand.

Without warning, she spritzes me with the heavy rose perfume she prefers. I wrinkle my nose, fighting to keep a sneeze from escaping as all hope of remembering that strange scent disappears.

"There, that's better," Merelda says with a nod before lifting her hand into the air as if its mere presence will make it easier to hear ... but then I hear it, too.

The sound of an approaching rider.

"Lord Payne has arrived," she informs me sharply.

"Remember to smile, girl ... and do exactly as you're told. Should you not gain Lord Payne's favor, I will see to it that you regret your very existence. Is that understood?"

I nod once, and she takes a deep breath before smoothing out her face and forcing a smile to her own lips. With one last inspection of me, she moves toward the stairs. I hesitate as I look toward Father's door, but Merelda makes an impatient sound, and I have no choice but to continue following her down the hall.

Male voices float up from below, and I have to fight off a wave of nausea as Merelda shoots me one last warning look before we descend the stairs.

My eyes immediately land on Lord Payne as he turns from Amadeus to look our way.

He's a wealthy man in the latter half of his life, his beady eyes trained on me as I give him a slight curtsy. His once dark hair has become thin and riddled with heavy silver threads that fail to make him look distinguished.

It's hard to ignore the velvet of his suit, imported to our little corner of the world from the capital, or the delicate golden thread that makes up the intricate designs.

There's no denying that the man is imposing, if not downright terrifying in his presence, as he approaches without a word, his eyes raking over every inch of my being.

I hate the way his gaze sticks to me. His calculating expression never changes, but from the way his eyes flash, I know he's satisfied with what he sees.

Merelda will be pleased with that, even if the very thought of it makes my skin crawl.

Lord Payne stops just a foot away from me, far too close for my comfort.

"Look at me, child."

Slowly, I lift my eyes to meet his, and I swear my heart nearly dies in my chest at the darkness I see within.

Reaching out, he runs a finger down my cheek, a thick iron ring in the shape of a snake wrapped around it.

I shudder at his touch, but he doesn't seem to notice or care.

"I'd like to take a closer look at the girl," Lord Payne says, turning toward Merelda.

"Of course, my lord, right this way," she agrees gesturing toward the front room. Lord Payne strides out of the entryway, as Merelda's sharp eyes find me. "You're to do exactly as he says, do you hear me? Exactly."

I open my mouth to answer just as Amadeus steps closer.

"My, isn't this exciting?"

"And you," Merelda starts, whirling on him with a sternness to her voice that I've never heard directed at her eldest son, "are going to stay right here."

"But I wanted to watch—"

"No." Amadeus looks shocked, if not more than a little hurt by his mother's tone as she grabs my wrist and drags me away. Stopping just outside the front room, she stops to give me a hard look. "Remember what I told you. Do not disappoint me."

With that she pushes me into the room, quickly pulling the door shut behind me.

Lord Payne doesn't turn to look at me right away, instead choosing to run his fingers along one of Father's bookshelves. I can hardly stand the sight of such a vile man touching his personal things, but I hold my tongue.

Finally, he glances over his shoulder at me before motioning toward the center of the room.

"Come closer, girl, and let me take a good look at you."

My stomach twists painfully, no doubt warning me not to obey this man, but I do as he says. Stepping toward me, he circles like a vulture eyeing up its prey.

"Bend over and touch your toes," Lord Payne says as he comes to a standstill behind me.

I slowly lean forward, my dress holding me in place by no small miracle, unsure of the reason for such a strange request. However, as soon as I'm bent over, I feel him grab my hips from behind to anchor me as he presses himself against me.

I barely have time to acknowledge the impropriety of what he's just done before he's stepped back.

"Hmm, and straighten again."

I'm all too happy to oblige this request as he rounds to face me. His eyes dip lower to the swell of my breasts.

"Perky little things, aren't they," he muses, reaching out to run a long nail along the very edge of where my breasts meet my neckline. "I suppose they'll do. Now, lift your skirts."

My heart pounds in my ears. Surely, I didn't hear him right.

"What?" I ask, the word barely a whisper.

"Lift your skirts. Don't make me ask again."

My hands clench, grabbing fistfuls of the brown fabric, but I refuse to obey.

"No."

The next thing I know, I find myself sprawled across the floor, my ears ringing from the force of his strike.

"I told you not to make me ask again," Lord Payne says, his voice barely audible above the din in my head.

Still in shock, I can barely make sense of what's happening as he moves to stand over me. Yanking my skirts, chemise and all, up over my hips, he smiles to himself as he leaves me utterly exposed to him.

"Very clean," he mutters to himself. "Unblemished, if not untouched."

I bite back tears, refusing to give him the satisfaction of knowing how great his offense is. I force myself to look away even as he continues to stare, cocking his head to one side in thought. Finally straightening, he steps back.

I just barely manage to regain enough control of myself to cover myself before he throws open the door.

"She'll do," he announces.

Merelda is all smiles and grace as she ushers him toward a chair, shooting a look my way in the process. My blood running cold within my veins, I want nothing more than to run from this room and never look back, but I have no choice but to join Merelda as she settles upon the faded settee.

I flinch as her hand comes to rest on my shoulder. I'm

sure it's meant as a display of motherly love for Lord Payne, but I can feel her holding me in place.

"About the betrothal," Merelda starts.

"I'd like to marry as soon as possible," he says, barreling over her. "Today, in fact."

If my stomach wasn't empty, I'd spew its contents all over them both at this. As it is, I'm simply left shaking beneath Merelda's hand.

"I appreciate your enthusiasm," Merelda tries again, giving him a small nod, "but I fear we can't allow that."

Lord Payne's eyes flash as he stares Merelda down.

"And why ever not?"

"The scandal," she answers hurriedly. "Just imagine the kind of scandal that would follow her. A rushed wedding will have the town talking, ruining the prospects of my own two sons in its wake."

Lord Payne considers her words for a moment before letting out a deep sigh.

"Of course, then what is it you suggest?"

"Well, there's also the small matter of her dowry. I can hardly imagine the loss our household will suffer with her gone. She cooks and cleans, tending to the many chores I simply cannot with an invalid husband. Without her, I fear the entire house might just fall into disarray."

"Nonsense, if that is all, then I'll see to it that her absence goes otherwise unnoticed by you or your household, Lady Godwin."

Of course, he would be the kind of man not to know our family name, if not misspeak it entirely on purpose.

Merelda pauses for a long moment before letting out a

small sob, the sound taking me entirely by surprise coming from her.

"I fear that I shall miss her dearly. She has been a great comfort to me, having no daughters of my own."

"Naturally, but I can assure you I will take great comfort from her, too."

Merelda's fingers tighten on my shoulder.

"Without her, I truly fear that I'll be left helpless and alone. A mother finds herself strangely reluctant to let her only daughter go, you see. Especially one as helpful as Hazel."

"I can assure you, Lady Godwin, that you will be well taken care of. Whether it be a large sum you require to hire help or anything else, you will want for nothing as long as Hazel and I are married."

Goodwin, not Godwin.

I have to grit my teeth together to keep myself from speaking out against his repeated offense over my father's good name.

"Oh, thank you, Lord Payne," Merelda simpers, tears springing to her eyes. "You are even more kind than I expected."

He lets out a low chuckle at this, and I'm almost impressed with my stepmother's negotiation. Not only has she found a way to get rid of me, but in the trade, she gains a new form of financial stability.

"Now, as I mentioned earlier, I'm eager to wed as soon as possible."

"Of course," Merelda says. "We'll need time to prepare a dress for her as well as all the necessary arrangements for such an affair. I believe two months should suffice."

"One."

Merelda pretends to consider his offer for a long moment, but I feel her hold on me relaxing.

Before she even opens her mouth to agree, I already know it's been decided.

As the two begin discussing some of the more minor details of the betrothal, my head swims. I'm to be married off to this disgusting monster in a month's time.

A single, solitary month.

In every way that matters, I feel like I've just been given a death sentence.

One month left to live.

9

HAZEL

Standing at Merelda's side, I train my eyes on the floor, gritting my teeth together as I wait for Lord Payne to finally leave. He pauses at the door, having just pulled on a pair of suede riding gloves.

"Oh, there's one more thing," he says, turning to close the distance between us. "Bring me a candle."

I half expect Merelda to balk at his demand, but she does as he says. Holding it out for him, Lord Payne removes the glove from one hand before twisting the snake-shaped ring from his finger.

Pinching it in his gloved hand, he holds it over the fire for several minutes as Merelda and I watch on in confusion. Then, without warning, he presses the head of the snake firmly against the swell of my breast.

I cry out in pain as the hot metal sears my skin. Merelda doesn't so much as flinch, even as he grabs me to anchor me in place, his eyes never leaving my face.

A minute later, he steps back, slipping the now cool ring back onto his finger as he examines the mark it left behind.

"Will that be all?" Merelda asks, her voice unwavering.

"For now," Lord Payne says, his eyes meeting mine, full of the dark promise that awaits me in a month's time.

My stomach knots as he bows his head once to Merelda before turning and finally disappearing into the night.

"I will not marry that man," I hiss, turning on Merelda the moment the door closes behind him.

"Don't be a fool, you ungrateful child," she replies. "It's already been agreed upon. Just be thankful that he's as rich as he is. You'll never want for anything, as long as you live."

"I'd rather *die* than marry a monster like him."

"You're a dramatic little thing, aren't you?"

"It's the truth," I reply. "I promise you; I will die before I ever marry Lord Payne."

"Then you'd better get started planning your own demise," she snaps back. "Mark my words, death will be your only escape from this marriage. So, tell me, how do you plan to throw yourself upon death's door? Can you imagine what your father would say if he could hear you now?"

Her cold laugh fills the room as she shakes her head at me, and I see the challenge in her eyes. I know I'll never be able to change her mind, but that doesn't mean I won't try to take fate into my own hands.

Anger burns through me, blurring my vision as I take in a deep breath. She may believe that she's the only one left who can make this decision, but I won't allow it.

Not as long as Father still draws breath. After what Lord

Payne did to me today, I know for certain this betrothal was *never* something he'd agree to.

Moving past my stepmother, I dart up the stairs.

Merelda makes no move to follow after me as I hurry down the hall toward Father's room.

I stop just outside the door, my heart pounding in my chest as I press a hand to the wood. Am I truly prepared to see whatever lies within?

Taking a deep, steadying breath, I close my eyes and push open the door.

The room is so dark that I have to blink several times to make sure I've actually opened my eyes. As my vision adjusts to the dimness of the room, I step inside. One step is all it takes for me to clearly see the severity of the situation.

Father is in bed, dwarfed by the blankets and pillows piled on top and around him. Behind a heavy metal grate, I can hear the crackle of a fire as it adds smoke and heat, but little light, to the already stiflingly hot room.

I take another step inside, straining my eyes in the dark as I draw closer to the bed. Father looks even worse than I'd expected. His skin is sallow, his face terrifying in its stillness. His eyes are closed, and for one terrible moment, I fear that he's no longer breathing.

Then I see his chest rise ever so slightly.

Gone is the strong man that my father once was, replaced by this fragile creature on the very brink of death.

What have they done to him?

What are they *doing* to him?

It makes no sense for the room to be so warm, the air

thick with sweat and smoke. He should be given fresh air and sunshine.

Standing beside the bed, I reach to take his hand. It's clammy with sweat as I squeeze it in my own. For the first time in my life, I note that his fingers are not stained with ink.

"Oh, Father," I breathe, dropping to my knees and pressing my forehead to the back of his hand, still clasped in my own. "Please. Please don't leave me. I can't bear the thought of life without you. There's still so much that I have to tell you."

As if on cue, everything I've held back comes tumbling from my lips. I tell him about Merelda's plan to wed me Lord Payne ... of how he treated me just moments ago. I hold nothing back as I explain what I've had to go through ever since he brought Merelda into our home, even going so far as to tell him of Amadeus' cruelty and Cyprian's strange kindness.

The words fall freely, my heart clearing itself of the weight it's held for so long, and I pray to the gods he can hear me. That he understands what I'm saying.

I need him to hear me ... I need him to stay.

Life without him here isn't one I want to find myself familiar with. He's still so young, at least it's always felt that way, and he has so much more life ahead of him. I'm sure of it.

I refuse to let Merelda and the doctor speak this curse of death over him. I refuse to let them destroy our future together.

"I promise you," I whisper, my eyes searching his face, "I

will find a way to save you, Father. I'll bring you back from death's door, even if it's the last thing I do."

The tears on my cheeks dry, leaving salty trails over my skin, as I watch Father's chest slowly rise and fall.

But he makes no other movement. Not even the fluttering of his eyes or the twitch of a finger to signal that he's heard what I've said.

Slowly, I rise to my feet.

Things are far worse than I could ever have imagined, but I will not allow my father to die so easily.

I don't care what I must do, but I'll find a way to save him. There must be someone out there who can help him. I won't waste what days he has left mourning him before he's even gone.

Determined to set out in search of help, I quietly slip back out into the hall.

I'm surprised Merelda isn't waiting just outside the door to scold or punish me. Even more surprising is the fact that she so easily allowed me to enter Father's room in the first place.

Unless she truly doesn't care what I do anymore. I suppose I have served my purpose now. In a month's time, she'll have more riches than she'll ever need, and I won't be a burden to her any longer.

Still, I pause and listen before making my next move.

The house is quiet, the only sounds the creaking of the wood as it settles around me. Night has long since fallen, but I know better than to hope or believe that my step family has retired for the day.

I'll have to wait until the darkest hour of night before I

slip from the house. Then, and only then, will it be safe for me to try to leave.

Back in my room, I bar the door before turning to look at what few possessions I have. Glancing down at myself, I hurry to rid myself of the dress Merelda put me in, letting it drop to a heap on the floor. Pulling on a more practical dress, I begin shoving random things into a small bag before finally glancing down at the pile of fabric laying on the floor.

As much as I hate to admit it, Merelda's dress is the nicest thing I own, and it may come in handy should I need to look ... presentable. Letting out a small sigh of defeat, I snatch the garment from the floor and fold it tightly before placing it inside my bag along with a pair of socks, a few candle stubs, and a tinderbox.

Taking a step back, I slowly realize this is nearly everything I own, aside from a few worn dresses, a coat, and my bed. Though, I suppose Merelda would argue the latter belongs to her now.

My heart skips a beat in my chest as I suddenly sink to my knees and pry back part of the wood floor, pulling out a small wooden box. Opening it, I run my fingers over the small packages within, each neatly tied with a red ribbon.

I'm more than a little tempted to undo all my packing and replace the items within with the contents of this box, but I know that would be foolish. Besides, it's not as if I won't return.

I have to return, for Father's sake.

Repeating this thought to myself, I carefully remove one of the packages. Pulling the ribbon loose I place it and the wax paper off to one side as I carry the small book that was tucked inside over to the window.

I spend the hours admiring the illustrations within by candle and starlight.

My eyelids grow heavy, and I briefly consider taking a nap, but decide against it. It would be all too easy for me to end up sleeping through the night. Tonight, of all nights, I can't allow exhaustion to get the better of me.

When I can no longer focus on the pages, I turn my eyes to the sky and stars. Time seems to slow, the seconds hesitant to slip into minutes as my impatience to get started grows.

My fingers tap anxiously on the windowsill, and soon I find myself pacing my tiny room.

It should be just a little while longer now.

Finally, I hear the creak of the stairs and then click of my stepmother's heels as she makes her way down the hallway and into Father's room. I'm surprised she's still staying with him, to be honest, but right now I welcome the knowledge.

At least I know where she is. My stepbrothers, on the other hand, are an entirely different story.

I decide to wait another half hour, hoping to give Merelda enough time to fall asleep. In the meantime, I carefully re-package the small book Father had given me for my eleventh birthday and place it and the box back into my secret hiding place.

At long last, the time has come.

Grabbing my small bag, I unbar my door and quietly pry it open to listen.

Nothing.

Slipping through the dark halls, I move past my step family's bedroom doors, carrying my shoes in one hand as I expertly navigate the creaking wood. I can't help but feel a little sad at the thought of leaving home, if only for a short while, as I make my way downstairs and to the back door.

As I sit to lace up my shoes, I glance around the kitchen one last time. Though Merelda has tried to make my life miserable, these halls, this home, still hold so much joy and love for me.

This is where I grew up.

Where I'd been held and comforted and loved by my parents.

This is my home, and no matter how hard Merelda might try, she can never take that away from me.

Getting to my feet, I take one more deep breath before pulling open the back door. I stare out into the dark night for a long minute before taking a step ... My first step toward saving Father.

With nothing but the stars and a new moon above me to light the way, the night is far darker than I'd anticipated.

A chilly breeze whips around me as I move silently from shadow to shadow. My heart pounds heavily in my chest at each creak of a tree or hoot of an owl ... as if at any second, my secret escape will be discovered.

Somehow, I manage to reach the broken fence without misfortune. Quickly pulling myself over it, I breathe a small sigh of relief. Though I'm still far from being safe, at least from here I can run.

Taking off down the hill, I make my way to the edge of our property. Clambering over the stone wall, I land in the tall grass beyond that marks my official success at leaving home behind.

Shadows stretch and loom before me, threatening to send my heart pounding from my chest, but I do my best to ignore them as I set off along the path toward town.

I'm nearly halfway there, too far from home yet not close enough to be near people, when I hear him.

"Well, what have we here."

My blood runs cold, stopping me in my tracks, one foot still lifted for the next step.

I swallow, closing my eyes for a moment, too afraid to peer into the darkness just behind me to confirm that the voice I just heard does, in fact, belong to my stepbrother.

That somehow, Amadeus has managed to find me, and that there's no one around to protect me from his lingering gaze or searching hands.

Slowly, I turn toward the sound, like prey cornered by a predator.

"Fate, it would seem, favors me having you, Hazel," Amadeus says, emerging from the shadows. "Again and again, I find you within my grasp."

"I-I'm betrothed."

Amadeus' face twists at this.

"I'll die before I let Payne take what is mine," he snarls. "I've spent far too long waiting for this moment to just let some old man slip in at the last moment. No, I'll have my way with you, first. Then you can go to your wedding bed thinking of me."

I stumble back a step, but it's too late. He's already on me, covering my body with his as he walks me backward.

My bag falls to the ground as he, yet again, shoves me up against the rough bark of a tree. The wind knocked out of me as his hands move along my dress, sending chills of foreboding racing across my skin and down my spine.

I shove my hands against his chest, but all I get in return is a hard slap across the face that sends my head spinning.

"Try that again, and I'll knock you out," he warns, one cold hand dipping beneath my skirts.

I want to close my eyes, to look away, but I don't.

His breathing is rough as his hand runs up my thigh, and I shiver as he draws closer to my core.

Should he ruin me tonight, I don't know what that would mean for my future. What little of it I have.

"Help!" I scream, the tail end of the word silenced as Amadeus clamps his other hand over my mouth.

"No one can hear you," he says, the hand beneath my skirts stilling for a moment as he leans in to whisper in my ear. "No one. Nothing but death will keep you from me."

Horror washes over me as I realize there's nothing I can do. My attempts to slip away are useless with him pinning me here.

I'm shorter than him, though that's no great compliment to his own height, and thinner too, thanks to his mother's careful rationing of my meals the past six or so years. Even if that wasn't the case, I'm not sure I'd have the strength to fight him off.

My stomach twists at the thought of what's to come next. Closing my eyes, I try to prepare myself for his touch as his fingers graze my innermost thigh.

But his touch never comes.

There's a heavy thud, and I slowly open my eyes to suddenly find myself no longer pinned against the tree.

It takes me a moment to adjust to the dim light before I realize Amadeus is lying in a crumpled heap at my feet. Standing just beyond, his chest heaving, is Cyprian.

Our eyes meet for a moment before I sag against the tree, relief pooling warm and welcome in my chest.

"I don't think he saw me," Cyprian says, breaking the stunned silence between us. "He was too focused on you. Are you all right, Hazel? Did he ..."

He trails off, unable to bring himself to finish his question, and I'm quick to shake my head.

"No, almost, but no."

"Good."

An uneasy quiet fills the space between us as our eyes slowly drop to Amadeus.

Blood pools on the back of Amadeus' head, nearly black in the dim light. Crouching, I reach to check the wound before stopping short.

The ground beneath Amadeus' head has begun to darken, becoming an ever-growing abyss in the night.

"There's too much blood," I breathe, glancing up at Cyprian as his eyes widen in panic.

It's only now that I realize what a mess he is. His white

shirt is splattered with blood, his hands bruised and swollen from fighting.

Standing, I move toward him, but he stops me, catching my hands in his before I can reach him.

"You have to go," he whispers.

"No, we'll deal with this together. If we can just explain ..." I trail off, realizing what a fool I am even to suggest it.

Cyprian starts to shake as he glances down at his brother's body. A growing sense of panic rises within me, threatening to overtake me, even as I try my best to push it down. As I try to ignore the way my own hands tremble.

"Hazel, I need you to listen to me," Cyprian begs, his voice low and warm in its concern for me. "You have to go. You can't be here when ... when they see what I've done. It'll only make things worse. Go, get as far away from here as you can."

"Come with me," I say, my eyes searching his face.

"No," he says, his brow furrowing. "I can't. They'll blame you for this. You know how my mother is. I need to stay. I have to find a way to fix this. Please, go. Save me by saving yourself. Get away from here, away from me as fast as you can, and never look back."

"Please, Cyprian, don't do this. We can run away together a-and ..."

Our eyes meet, and a tear finds its way down my cheek as I realize this is goodbye. It doesn't matter who was at fault here, someone will have to pay for the shedding of Amadeus' blood. Whether I stay or go, I will be the one blamed. Merelda will stop at nothing until I've been brought to justice.

Still, I can't just leave him here.

"Please," I whisper one last time.

"No. If I left with you, it would only put you in far worse danger," Cyprian says, lifting one hand to gently caress my cheek. "I can't do that to the girl I've loved since I first laid eyes on her."

I blink up at him, taken aback by his confession as he reaches into his pocket and pulls out the small book my father gave him so long ago.

"Cyp—"

"Take this," he says quickly, pressing it into my hand. "Take this, and don't look back. Now, Hazel, run!"

I still hesitate, uncertain, before slowly backing away. My heart aches as I take one last look at Cyprian and then turn on my heel to race off into the night.

Tears fall freely down my cheeks as I leave Cyprian standing there alone in the dark, hovering over Amadeus, blood staining his boots. I stumble over rocks in my haste to get away, but I drag myself up and push myself to continue. I can't stop, no matter how badly my legs ache or my lungs burn.

Failing to escape would only mean Cyprian's sacrifice was in vain.

Reaching the edge of town, I stop to catch my breath while I'm still hidden within the confines of the forest. I glance about, my mind racing to come up with some kind of plan.

All I know is that going into town would be a mistake. I need to get as far away from here as I can, and I can't risk anyone seeing me or being alerted to the direction I'm traveling.

My eyes trail over the imposing silhouette of the dense forest contrasted heavily by the warm, softly lit buildings of the town it surrounds.

I'd never ventured further than this when it came to the forest. It only grew darker and more wild from here, and had always been an imposing force standing at the very edge of my little world ...

But perhaps, just this once, it will become my refuge and grant me the safety that I so desperately need.

10

HAZEL

Darting across the road, I veer left, and straight into the depths of the trees beyond. The forest was my best hope, my best chance of protection from anyone else who might be lurking in the shadows ... or anyone who might come looking for me.

I can't help but wonder if Merelda will hunt me down herself. Perhaps she'll place a bounty on my head, or worse still, send Lord Payne to drag me back.

My steps quicken at this thought, but with each step further into the forest, the dim light from the stars above fades until I'm forced to slow.

Branches scrape over my skin, tugging at my dress and hair. Closing my eyes to protect them, I use my hands to navigate through the thicket I seem to have found myself in.

My foot catches in a tangle of wiry vines, and I let out an annoyed sigh as I struggle to disentangle myself.

Finally breaking free of the thicket, I struggle to hold

back tears as I realize I can still hardly see a thing. Pressing onward, I check each step before taking it, my hands held out in front of me to keep me from running into anything.

I don't know how long I continue on like this. All I know is that my going is slow.

Too slow.

Especially if Cyprian and Amadeus have been discovered. I need to put as much distance between them and myself as possible, but at this rate, I'll never manage it.

Squinting once again into the pitch-black darkness, I curse myself for dropping my bag, and with it my tinderbox and candles. If only I'd been more careful to avoid Amadeus, I'd now be able to navigate these trees.

I wouldn't even need to. If Amadeus hadn't caught me, I wouldn't be escaping through the forest while he lies dead on the ground.

Looking up through the thick foliage overhead, I let out a small cry of frustration at the moonless sky.

"I need help. Just a little light, anything ... please."

I sink to my knees in defeat, just as something flickers into view up ahead. My heart skips a beat as I lean forward to push several branches aside, and the light brightens further.

It's just a small pinprick of warm golden light, but it's more than enough to give me hope.

"Thank you," I whisper in silent prayer as I scramble back to my feet.

Cautiously, I make my way toward it, the light growing brighter as the darkness of the forest slowly gives way to it the closer that I get.

Finally, after pushing my way through a particularly thick set of bushes, I stumble out into a small clearing. There, sitting in the middle of the dark forest is a tiny cottage. I frown as I stare at it, wondering what I should do next.

The clearing is overflowing with wildflowers of every size, shape, and color, many of which I've never seen before. The cottage itself has thick winding vines twisting up and over it.

Everything about this place feels strange, and yet, somehow familiar ... as if I've seen this place before. The air is saturated with the crisp scent of flowers and starlight. As I take another step into the clearing, a warm breeze brushes past me, playing at the lengths of my skirts as my eyes widen in wonder.

Lazy fireflies drift past me, making the whole scene feel that much more magical. Turning my gaze back to the cottage, my eyes catch on the lantern hanging by the door. That must be the light that drew me here.

How did I not know a place like this existed so close to home?

I stand in the midst of the wildflowers, contemplating my next move. Firelight flickers in one of the small paned windows, half hidden in vines, but I can't see anything else from here.

There's no movement, no sign that anyone has spotted me, but that doesn't mean the cottage is empty. Before I've even come to a decision, I realize I'm already moving closer, as if the cottage itself is pulling me toward it.

At least anyone who lives this far out of town is unlikely

to have heard anything about Amadeus or the girl suspected of bludgeoning him over the head. Perhaps, whoever is here, will at least be willing to point me in the right direction, if not give me a candle to help light the way.

Approaching the arched door, I stop to listen for the sounds of someone moving about inside, but it's quiet. For a second, I contemplate lifting the lantern from its hook and simply disappearing into the forest with it, but the very thought makes me sick with guilt.

So, I do the only thing I can.

My knock is quiet, but it still seems to shatter the peace of the clearing. I anxiously wait for a long moment, but nothing happens.

I should have known better. It's far too late for anyone to be awake, let alone willing to open their door to a perfect stranger, especially here.

I'm just about to walk away when I hear the soft shuffle of feet approaching.

My heart skips a beat as I take a step back. I glance over my shoulder, trying to gauge whether or not I stand a chance of running away, of fleeing before I'm caught out here alone.

As far as I know, the cottage could hold a fate even worse than the one Amadeus or Lord Payne promised.

This was a mistake. I should have known better than to approach a strange house, especially one set in the middle of a dark forest.

I start to turn, but before I can flee, the door creaks open, and I find myself caught.

Slowly, I look back to find a woman peering out at me. I

start, blinking in surprise as I recognize her as the strange woman from the tavern.

The woman Cyprian had called a witch.

She stares at me in silence for a long moment before finally opening the door wider. I hesitate when she simply steps aside and nods once for me to enter.

My feet carry me inside as if they have minds of their own, and the strange woman shuts the door behind me.

She ushers me into the main room of the cottage, and I can't help but take it all in. It's a clean and cozy little space, well-loved from the worn rug and soft furniture. At the back of the room, a rocking chair sits next to a crackling fire, a book and steaming mug set on a small table to one side of it.

Clearly, I've interrupted her evening, despite how late it is.

I let my eyes take everything in before turning back toward the woman. Questions pile themselves atop my tongue, but she silences them with a single look.

"Sit," she tells me, her voice firm but kind, "and I'll put the kettle on."

She gestures toward the fire, and I make my way over to it. Passing an overstuffed bookshelf and wooden table filled with an odd assortment of jars and dried herbs, I settle myself on a small footstool facing the rocking chair.

Staring at the fire, exhaustion begins to worm its way back into me. Leaning forward, I prop my head up in my hands as my eyelids begin to grow heavy.

"Here you are, dear."

I'm startled back awake, as I look up to find the woman

standing next to me, offering me a steaming mug of my own.

"Thank you," I say, accepting the mug as she settles onto the rocking chair. I stare down at the swirling tea leaves as steam wafts around my face, wondering how much I should tell her of my predicament. "I suppose you're wondering why I'm here."

"You're here for help," she replies.

Blinking, I glance back up at her.

"How did you know?"

"Why else would a young maiden such as yourself be wandering the depths of the forest on a moonless night?"

A small laugh escapes me at this.

Of course. It must have been obvious to her that I was in desperate need of help the moment she opened her door. Living all the way out here, she probably doesn't get many visitors this late at night, unless they truly need her help.

It certainly wouldn't take supernatural powers to deduce that from my current state.

"You're right," I admit, shaking my head as I let out a small snort. "And to think I almost believed Cyprian when he said you were a witch."

"Oh, but he's not wrong about that."

I balk at this, nearly spilling the piping hot tea all over myself in the process.

"What?"

She gives me a kind smile as she reaches out to help right the trembling mug in my hands.

"I mean you no harm, child," she quickly reassures me. "In fact, it is I who owes you a favor."

"I-I'm afraid I don't understand."

"There is not much to understand," she continues. "Once, many moons ago now, your father helped me when I was in desperate need and all but him turned a blind eye. Now, I should like to repay his kindness by helping you."

Her mention of Father brings a smile to my face.

I certainly didn't expect my plans to go smoothly, but this is an unexpected turn of luck. If she can help me save Father, then I'll be forever in her debt, and gladly so.

Witch or not.

"Father—"

"I do not have the means to save him," she interjects, as if reading my mind. "Unfortunately, the magic that requires is far beyond my skill. However, I do know of ... *someone* who may be able to help."

Something about the way she says this has the hair on the back of my neck rising to stand on end.

"Who?" I ask, swallowing past my unease.

"I should warn you, it won't be easy," she says, ignoring my question. "And you'll have to leave tonight, and soon, if you are to have any hope of finding him in time."

Her eyes glaze over as they drift from my face to the window behind me. A small frown tugs at her mouth, her eyes unblinking as she stares out into the forest beyond her cottage.

I slowly turn to follow her gaze, but see nothing more than the flicker of fireflies and the darkness that lies beyond. I open my mouth to question her, only to realize I still don't know this woman's name.

"Yes. Yes, you must leave now," she says, her eyes blinking back to focus. "Quickly, if you want any chance of you finding him, you must do so tonight, while the moon is still cloaked in shadow."

I'm confused, but as she stands, I do the same. The witch takes back my still-full mug before crossing over to a table.

I watch as she collects several more items from various places around the room. Her lips move in unspoken words as she turns back to me, motioning for me to join her.

"You must head directly north," she says, pushing several packets and jars into my hands before muttering to herself and taking them all back. "Directly north. Never veering from your course."

"How will I know if I'm heading the right way?"

"You will feel it in your bones. In the air you breathe, and the very earth that rises beneath your feet," she tells me. "Oh, and it'll be cold. Terribly, unforgivably cold ... You'll need a cloak."

The way she says this last part nearly draws a surprised laugh from my lips.

"A cloak?"

"Yes, here," she says, bustling about me before thrusting a worn magenta cloak into my arms. "Now, hurry along, dear. You mustn't delay any longer."

Ushering me toward a back door, I nearly stumble over my own feet as I step back into the clearing. She gives me a good look, her eyes trailing over me, before nodding.

"But, where do I go?"

Her eyes glaze over again at my question, lifting toward the forest. Slowly, she points, directing me out into the inky blackness beyond the clearing. I stare at it for a long moment, before turning back to face her.

Grabbing my hand, the witch pulls a small crystal from her skirt pocket before thrusting it into my hand and folding my fingers over it.

"Follow the cold and the shadows of night," she says cryptically. "The crystal will help guide your path. May each of your steps be certain and true."

With that, she turns back toward her cottage and the warmth within.

"Wait!" I reach out to stay her a moment longer.

Her eyes turn to meet mine as she raises an eyebrow in silent question. Swallowing my uncertainty yet again, I force one last question past my lips.

"Who am I looking for?"

The witch glances nervously over my shoulder before finding me again.

"He is called many things," she answers, "but you will call him The Bargainer."

"But how will I know who he is?"

"Trust me. You will know him when you see him, child. Now, go."

With that, she gives my shoulder a gentle push, and for the second time tonight, I find myself with nowhere to go but the forest.

11

HAZEL

I step away from the cottage, wrapping the heavy cloak around me, as I hear the soft click of the door closing behind me.

Taking a deep breath, I square my shoulders and set off across the clearing in the direction the witch had pointed. If what she's told me is true, if this person can truly save my father, then I have no choice but to find him.

Pausing at the edge of the clearing, I glance back at the cottage one more time only to have my heart skip a beat in my chest.

From this angle, the strange little cottage in the woods looks exactly like the one I'd painted back in Father's workshop. It must be a sign. That, or this is all just some strange nightmare that I've yet to wake up from.

Holding onto hope, I turn back toward the forest and plunge into the inky woods beyond.

As soon as I've left the clearing, the light behind me

disappears, throwing me into darkness as a cool wind whips around my face.

I'm just starting to wonder how I'm ever going to find my way, when I feel a warm tingling work its way up my arm. Glancing down, I slowly open my fist to reveal the small crystal laying in the palm of my hand.

It glows a soft pink, emitting just enough light for me to see one step ahead. I can't help but admire it, my mind almost refusing to accept what it sees.

There's no way to explain it other than magic.

Real *magic.*

If only Cyprian were here to see this. I can almost see the way his eyes would light up, the way he'd smile at me ...

Blinking back a sudden wave of tears, I quickly quiet these thoughts, pushing them deep down into the recesses of my mind.

I don't have time for this, not now.

I have to focus.

To hold onto hope of a future.

Clinging tightly to the glowing crystal, I hold it high, but see nothing but a pitch-black void in every direction.

Feeling more than a little overwhelmed, I make the mistake of forgetting everything the witch had told me as soon as I try to take my first step. Instantly, I find myself sinking into the ground as I scramble to pull myself back. I just barely manage not to topple headlong into the dark forest as I throw my balance backward instead.

Suddenly, I realize the light around me is fading and lurch forward just in time to snatch the little pink crystal before it's swallowed by the forest floor.

Dirty and my breathing heavy, I pull my legs to my chest as I take a moment to collect myself. I close my eyes, re-focusing on what the witch had told me.

My steps must be certain and true, I have to know I'm going the right way. No veering off course, even by mistake.

One wrong move could prove fatal, as I nearly just discovered.

Still more than a little shaken, I force myself back onto my feet and try again.

Much more carefully this time, I forge my way deeper and deeper into the forest, testing my steps first just as the witch had instructed.

At least the witch had been right about me simply knowing the right way to go, though I wish she'd been a little clearer about how I would know.

It isn't long before I come up with a process, sweeping one foot out before me until a deep chill washes over me, racing down my spine and, quite literally, into the very depths of my being. Even then, I'm wary as I slowly shift more and more of my weight forward.

With each step in the right direction, the ground grows harder beneath my feet, and the air around me colder. Clutching the cloak tighter, my fingers nearly frozen in a cage around the precious crystal, I push onward.

The trees begin to thin, their branches growing bare as the path becomes littered with dead leaves and branches instead.

The darkness seems to become thicker and heavier as it begins to weigh on me with each step forward. Soon, even the glow from the crystal in my hand is barely visible as I continue to force myself to place one foot in front of the other.

My lungs begin to burn as the air grows frosty within them, and a thin mist creeps in around me, welcoming me to this new part of the forest.

Suddenly, the world around me goes quiet, and I still. Hardly daring to breathe, I wait and listen for some sign of life. For a bird to call out its song, or a twig to snap beneath a rabbit's foot.

But there is no sound.

It's as if the forest has swallowed everything save for my own ragged breathing.

The air is almost too thick to breathe, and appears to be dripping with tiny glistening icicles as I glance about.

I pull the cloak tighter around my shaking shoulders, though there's little warmth left in it.

My feet drag as I push myself to continue, and soon, even my own breath seems to form hanging icicles in the air as it leaves me. The wetness of my mouth and eyes begin to freeze over, blurring my vision and chapping my lips.

I have to blink repeatedly in an attempt to clear my vision. Three steps more is all it takes before even that won't stop the icicles from blinding me. Unable to blink the frost from my eyes, I close them until all I can see is a sliver of light through my eyelashes.

I can make nothing of the shapes ahead, and I'm forced to rely on nothing but the knowing in my bones, and the feel of the earth beneath my boots instead.

Frost collects on my lashes and across my skin as I press on. My breathing has turned into short gasps of pain.

And yet, I don't give up.

A bitter wind picks up, howling in my ears, screaming at me to turn back before it's too late. I tuck my chin against it, but even that does little to bring me relief.

The cold weighs on me, pressing against my ribs with each inhale of ice. It's begun to feel as if my heart and soul are being squeezed from me. What I'd give for a breath of air that isn't sharp with ice crystals.

Still, I press on.

Then, I hear a voice. It's as sharp as the ice that clings to me, cutting through the howl of the wind, despite my ears not being able to make sense of it.

I pause, shivering as I pry my eyes open, despite the frost having nearly frozen them shut.

Suddenly, the wind is gone.

Silence presses in as the world seems to be frozen in time. Crystals of ice hang unmoving in the air, shifting only with the exhale of my breath or the turning of my head as I search for the voice in the darkness.

"What brings you here, little one?" the voice comes again, clear and colder than the very air around me. It pierces my heart like an icy dagger, stealing what little air I have left from me.

I've never heard anything like it.

Part of me longs to hear it again, to feel the edge of this being's voice cut across my skin, sharper than a blade, and stronger than steel ... and yet, I know I shouldn't want that.

"Speak," the voice commands, terrible in its beauty.

"The Bargainer," I rasp, peering into the darkness around me as I try to see who I'm speaking to. "He is who I'm searching for. I must speak with him."

The crystal barely produces enough light for me to see past the glint of the frozen droplets, the shadows beyond cloaking the voice in darkness.

The voice says nothing, the stretching silence settling as a lead weight of disappointment in my stomach.

If this man isn't the one that I seek, then I don't know how I can continue on. I'll have failed in my quest to save my father.

Unable to accept this outcome, I open my mouth again.

"Are you him? Are you the one they call The Bargainer?"

There's a brief pause that has my heart racing in my chest before he answers, "I am known by many names, little creature, but yes, that is one of them."

My relief upon hearing this is immediate.

I straighten, squinting out through the glittering ice as I try to make him out, but the shadows refuse to open up to me. A surge of hope drives me forward another step, my heart pounding in my chest.

"Please," I say, nearly choking on the word. "Please, I wish to make a deal. A bargain with you. It's important."

Again, the voice remains silent, and I can't help but wonder what I've done wrong.

Finally at my breaking point, I let out a small sob, but the moment my tears start to burn the back of my eyes, they turn to ice.

I let out a hiss of pain as I collapse to my knees. Pressing the base of my palms to my eyes in an effort to warm them, I will myself to calm down.

I can't give up now, not when I'm so close to getting what I've come for. If the witch believes that he can help me, then I have to trust that he will. That he is the one I've been searching for.

"Please, I'll do anything."

The shadows let out a sigh that wraps around me like a bitter wind, bringing an even deeper chill to my skin. Still, hope dares to sprout in my chest.

"You should turn back, little one. You know not what you ask for."

"Please, I cannot. I need your help."

"Turn back."

"No," I answer, putting as much force as I can behind the word, "not before you've heard my plea, or do you not abide by your own name?"

I don't know what makes me say these words, but something about them makes the very atmosphere tremble around me.

The silence is almost ear-splitting as I worry that I've just offended him beyond repair.

"Please," I try, one last time. "Please, it's urgent."

"Is that so?"

All I can do is nod my head.

I wish that the air around us was less frigid. That I could at least look upon him as I beg him to save Father. As things are, it seems that the gods are more intent on showing me just how insignificant I am in this man's presence.

"Very well, but you must look upon me before you make your request."

This startles me, and I worry I won't be able to meet his condition as I force my eyes open wider, wincing at the ice that stabs me.

Peering into the darkness, I try desperately to find him ... to focus on the shifting shadows, wondering which of them might belong to him. I swear my mind is playing tricks on me as they all blur together, and I let out a groan of frustration.

Surely, I cannot have come this far just to fail now.

I'm starting to think all is lost when a figure steps from the shadows that part like ink before me.

Blinking, my eyes widen, unable to do anything but stare as he moves into the faint glow of the crystal. I have to crane my neck to look up at him as he towers above me.

My heart skips as I take in the terrifying skull-masked face of this being, my mind no longer accepting he is simply a man.

Swirling darkness cloaks him like a living creature as he bends down toward me.

My entire body begins to shake as his deep black eyes peer out from the mask to meet mine, and I swear he sees into the very depths of my soul as I let out a gasp of surprise.

Unblinking, he makes no further sound or movement as I continue to stare at him. It suddenly strikes me that he's probably waiting for me to make my plea.

My mouth opens, but at first, no words come out.

Frowning, I suddenly clutch at my chest as it feels like the last bit of warmth slips from my body.

I let out a small, shuddering gasp just as the remainder of my strength seeps from me.

"Father," I whisper, the word nearly dying on my lips, before complete and utter darkness finally takes me.

12

THE BARGAINER

F ather?
	I frown, staring down at the girl's crumpled body for a moment before couching to prod her gently with a gloved finger.

She does not so much as twitch or acknowledge my touch, her face still and her breathing shallow, and after only speaking that one word.

Father.

It makes no sense. I am no one's father, least of all to this frail little creature lying before me.

Straightening, I let out a deep sigh, my shadows swirling around me in agitation.

What am I supposed to do now?

Cocking my head to one side and then the other, I nudge her with the toe of my boot. Still, she does not move.

Her eyes are closed, ice already frosting over her lashes. I cannot simply leave her here, and yet I do not know what else to do.

Judging from the fragility of her breaths, she is unlikely to wake again if she remains where she is. She will die if I leave her here, and it is not yet her time.

Besides, she did ask for The Bargainer, and a deal has yet to be reached between us. A bargain yet to be decided upon.

Of course, I could simply choose to walk away. There would certainly be consequences for doing so, least of all her untimely death, but is the alternative worth the effort?

And then again, there is that altogether confounding matter of her last uttered word. My fingers twitch at my sides as my eyes trail over her tiny body.

"Damn it," I sigh deeply, realizing I have no real choice in the matter, not if I want to continue to live in peace for the foreseeable future.

I can almost hear the shrill voices of the Fates already, berating me as they are forced to untangle and pull apart the threads that led her here. The headache that alone would cause is motivation enough for me to kneel and reach for her.

It seems I have no choice but to bring her home with me and see to it that she does not die before we can reach an agreement.

I am careful to readjust my outfit before reaching for the girl. Should she come into contact with my skin, even just for a moment, then all will be for naught.

Lifting her into my arms, I clench my jaw in pain as the warmth of her body penetrates me, sending a strange shiver down my spine and into the very depths of my being.

I had almost forgotten what living creatures felt like.

Glancing down at her tiny face, I cannot help but feel like I have seen her somewhere before. Though it strikes me as odd that I recognize her at all. Human faces being what they are, and all.

Furrowing my brow in thought, it slowly dawns on me where I have seen this human before.

It was the tavern.

I had stepped in for a moment to watch and listen to the humans and their tales, a brief respite from the dead bodies I had spent the day dealing with. Though, I suppose in a way, they are not altogether different.

Perhaps that is why I frequent such places.

Most of the souls there that night were simply part of the living dead as they drank their souls into blurry oblivion. And, unless one drinks themselves to death, it is the closest I can stand when it comes to being around humans.

Living ones, that is.

Except for her.

She had been sitting alone, when she suddenly glanced my way.

I thought it curious at the time, but as beautiful as her blue eyes had sparkled in the dim light, they were mortal still. There was no way she could have known I was there, let alone see me.

And yet, I had felt oddly exposed by the way her eyes had searched the shadows.

Her soul had called out to me, but its song was different.

It was not a song of death.

Unlike the others, whose souls sing the slow tune of

131

their lives, filling my ears with the melody of their final hour, hers was a song I had never heard before.

One I could not quite understand. And one I will never understand if we remain here, where souls are silenced.

I suddenly realize that the girl's body has grown stiffer in my arms. I will not get any answers if I keep her out in this cold any longer.

First warmth, and then we can finish our deal. Perhaps then, I will finally understand what her soul was singing to me that night.

Turning, I start to step away just as something catches the corner of my eyes. Looking down at the ground just to one side of where the girl collapsed, I see a small book.

Crouching as I cradle the girl against my chest, I pick it up. It fits neatly in my palm, the cover worn and faded from use, and yet still captivating in its beauty. Tucking it into my shirt, I rise again.

Tightening my hold on the girl, I turn once again and move deeper into the inky shadows as they swirl up around me. Embracing the utter darkness, I slip quickly through the nothingness, savoring it as together we become all and nothing before it finally releases me, and I step out into my own realm.

Kicking open the heavy black doors, I am greeted by a cavernous abyss of an entryway.

Stepping inside, the emptiness of the palace presses in

on me, as it always does, and I allow myself to bask in it as I stride through the quiet halls.

I cannot remember a time when another being was here with me.

Until now, that is.

I glance down at the girl. Her skin is pale, and the blue tinge that's crept into her lips almost makes it look like death has already claimed her. I cannot stop myself from admiring how much death seems to suit her.

And yet, that is not why she is here.

Striding further into my palace, I carry the girl toward one of the main rooms, the click of my boots against the obsidian echoing through the vast halls.

The room is empty, save for a black settee trimmed in gold, and, of course, a large fireplace. Tearing the wet cloak from her shoulders, I toss it aside before gently placing the girl down on the settee. She looks so beautiful in her stillness that I find it hard to look away.

But I do.

Turning, I step toward the lifeless fireplace. Kneeling before it, I realize that it has been centuries, if not millennia, since I last had to worry about lighting a fire. I scowl at it for a long moment before rising to my feet and making my way to the kitchen to get a tinderbox.

Returning to the cold sitting room with a tinderbox as well as several furs in hand, I set to work warming the girl back from the brink of death.

Wrapping her in the furs, I turn toward the fireplace once again with a heavy sigh.

I set my jaw as I struggle to bring the fire to life. As soon as it finally takes, I step back quickly from the burst of heat.

Watching from the darkest corner of the room, I wait for the girl to wake.

The fire casts a soft glow over her, almost instantly bringing color back to her cheeks. Her lips slowly changing from blue to purple to a delicate rose.

And then I hear it, that same strange song faintly calling to me.

Relief washes over me, and I am not quite sure what to make of the sensation. Shaking the feeling, I turn my thoughts elsewhere.

I wonder where this small fragile creature came from, and what it is she intends to bargain for.

I cannot remember the last time someone came searching to make a deal with me. It was always me having to go to them, and they were always criminals. Corrupt royals or nobles looking to climb the ladder. Greedy men and women eager to get their hands on what others had, without having to earn it for themselves.

They were always selfish people who had no interest in anything but themselves.

And yet, this girl seems to be none of those things. Neither corruption nor greed mar her features.

So, what is it that she wants?

I cannot help the way I find myself admiring her delicate features, and the beauty buried within them. The soft rise and fall of her body buried beneath the furs.

I almost want to feel the pain of her heat seeping into

me as it had earlier, and I find myself taking a step toward her before I stop myself.

I frown, unsure of what to make of this strange desire to draw near her, to hold her in my arms again. The very thought of her warmth should be off-putting to me, and yet, it is not.

Sighing deeply, I shake my head, chalking it up to curiosity and my desire to study her. There is something different about her, and I intend to find out exactly what that is.

Besides, it is not often that I find myself spending time in the company of the living, and never before has one entered my home.

Perhaps I have spent too many years amongst the dead, too many years wandering these halls alone. Already, I can sense that her mere presence alone has changed the very essence of my palace.

The air is shifting, melting, and I do not know what to make of it.

Perhaps I should send her on her way before she ruins everything that I have worked so long for. But then again, what harm can a mere human truly do?

No, I am not quite ready to have her gone from here. Not until I can glean my own answers from her.

Even if it means I and my halls must endure a little change.

13

HAZEL

My eyes flutter open, the weight of my lids heavy as I glance about.

This place is unfamiliar to me, and no matter how hard I try, I can't remember how I got here. Let alone where *here* is.

Slowly, I push back the heavy furs covering my body and take in the roaring fire. It's warm, but does little to fight off the true chill or shadows that seem to fill the place.

Cold and dark, the room itself almost seems as if it's been created by that same inky darkness that I'd encountered in the forest. The same presence that still seems to linger in the corner of my eye.

Frowning, I turn back to look at the fire. Even it seems wrong. I'm nowhere near as warm as I should be given my proximity to it. And the way its flames lick at the wood, the strange blue-tinged hue ... I've never seen a fire burn like this before.

It's almost as if it isn't burning at all.

I rub my eyes, but the dream persists. Turning, I suddenly realize the shadow lurking in the corner of my vision isn't a figment of my imagination, but a man.

My heart leaps into my throat as I scramble back on the couch, drawing the furs and my knees up to my chest in the process. The shadows around him swirl, and though he doesn't move, I can feel his eyes on me.

Slowly, he cocks his skull-masked face to one side.

"Are you afraid, little one?"

I blink at him, unsure of how to answer him. But how can I when I don't know who he is?

Perhaps I hit my head harder than I thought, one glance around this room. One glance at him and the darkness that clings to him should be enough to send me running for my life.

And yet, it only makes me more curious about him.

"Should I be?" I finally answer.

He says nothing, watching me for a long moment, and I do my best to hold his gaze. It's not easy staring into the endless abyss of his black eyes. They unsettle me to no end, but I refuse to release myself from them.

Tentatively, he takes a step forward, and I involuntarily stiffen.

"I suppose that depends," he says, his deep voice is quiet and yet fills the room with its presence. "Tell me, what is the deal you wish to make with me?"

I frown as I search my mind. My memories seem faded, as if shrouded in a heavy fog ... Closing my eyes, it takes a long moment before my heart pangs with remembrance.

"Father," I gasp, opening my eyes, "I need help saving my father's life."

The masked stranger eyes me before asking, "What makes you think that I am capable of helping you with such a thing as that?"

There's an edge to his voice, but I don't let it scare me.

"I don't know," I start, my words falling quiet as I realize that I have no real way of answering his question. "I wouldn't have come to you, except that I was told to."

"Who told you?"

"A witch. I'm afraid I don't know her name. She said you could help me. That if I went north, and didn't stray from the path, I'd find the one who could save my father."

His skepticism is obvious, despite his face being hidden, and I frown as I try to think of a way to prove what I'm saying is true. I don't know why, but it suddenly seems important to do so.

"She has a cottage in the middle of the woods," I say, racking my mind for details about her appearance, but coming up short. "I must admit, I don't remember what she looks like, but she's the one who gave me the pink cloak and crystal."

Suddenly remembering the crystal, I realize it's still clasped in my hand. I extend my hand to show him, only to find the crystal is no longer pink and has lost its soft glow. All that is left is a small, obsidian stone in its place.

I stare at it in disbelief for a long moment before lifting my eyes back to the man.

"Ravynn," he mutters.

Hope rises in my chest at this, realizing this must be the witch's name.

"So, is it true?" I ask. "Can you save my father?"

"Of course, I can," he says with a deep sigh, "but saving a life requires the greatest cost of any bargain one can make."

"I don't care," I say quickly. "I'll do anything, give you anything, to save him. Please."

He watches me for a long minute. I can feel his eyes moving across my face, searching for something, though what, I do not know.

Hope and quiet desperation well up inside me as I wait, clutching the furs with both hands to keep myself from doing something foolish like running to prostrate myself at his feet.

If he says no, I don't know what I'll do.

"To save your father's life," he says slowly, his voice careful and measured, "you must offer your own in exchange."

It takes a moment for my mind to process what he's just said.

"If I accept, then he'll survive?"

He's quiet for a second as if unsure whether or not to continue.

"It is not quite as simple as that," he says. "The deal must be struck before first light, while the moon has yet to be re-birthed, but the deal will only come into effect once the moon has completed a full cycle."

My heart sinks at this. A whole month, he could be dead by then.

"And if he dies before then?"

Again, he hesitates before answering, "He will not, as long as you remain here with me during that time. Your life force will slowly feed your dying father until the deal is complete."

I wrap my arms around myself in comfort as I give myself a moment to think. I hadn't anticipated having to give up what little remains of my time with Father as well as my own life to save him.

"And if I choose not to stay here with you, then what happens?"

"Then you will have to hope that he has enough strength to survive until the next new moon on his own."

I suppose I should be grateful that at least I have a choice when it comes to being this man's captive, though it comes at the risk of my father dying.

"However," he continues, almost as if reading my mind, "should you choose not to remain here, if your father dies before our deal is complete, your life will not be forfeit."

"And if I die here? Before our deal is complete," I ask warily.

He snorts softly.

"Impossible, I will not allow that to happen."

"How can you be sure?"

"You have my word."

I pause for a moment, contemplating my choice. It seems unwise to stay here with this man, after all, I do not know what this strange man's word is worth. Yet, I'm unwilling to put my father's life in fate's hands, given how last I saw him.

Father is dying, and despite the fear that threatens to

pull me apart, and the worry that this may still end terribly, I know what I must do.

"I'll do it," I say, meeting the dark pools with the skulled mask. "I accept your offer. I will stay here until the deal is complete, and my father's life is saved."

The shadows are quiet for a long moment, the man's eyes never once leaving my face.

I do my best to pull myself up, to not let my lips quiver or my eyes dart about. There is a part of me that suddenly feels trapped. A part, deep down, that almost wants to take back what I've just agreed to.

The very thought of staying here in this lifeless place with him makes my skin crawl ... though I'm not sure if it's from dread or relief.

"Very well, then our deal is struck," he says with a nod. "You will remain here until the next new moon, at which point you will relinquish your life to me in exchange for his."

My throat is suddenly thick with emotion.

I can almost see Father's disapproval over what I've just done. I know he would never ask this of me, let alone accept this sacrifice if he had any choice in the matter.

He wouldn't want me to be so quick to throw my life away. Though, without him, there wasn't much left to live for.

I'd have been married off to Lord Payne, if I wasn't made to pay for what happened to Amadeus first. I shudder at the thought of both these things. No, I've made the right choice for us both.

Father will live, and through my sacrifice, he can continue to make the world a better, more hopeful place.

I take a deep breath, waiting for a long moment for something to happen. For some sign that our deal is more than just words. Perhaps, for my soul to feel bound to magic.

Something.

But I don't feel any different than I did before.

"Come," my new master says, "I will show you around."

Numbly, I shift the furs from me and get to my feet. Slipping the black crystal into my skirts, I move away from the warmth of the fire, and a deep shiver instantly besets me.

"You are cold."

"I'm fine, thank you."

I can feel his eyes on me, the concern in them as I pretend to be unaffected by the unnerving chill of this place.

Despite the cold and shadows, I find myself eager to see the rest of his home. If I'm going to spend the rest of my life here, I might as well make the most of it. And, judging from the size of this one room, there will be a lot to explore.

"Hmm."

He says nothing else as he sweeps past me, the living shadows that cling to him swirling around his feet as he opens the door. I'm quick to follow after him, my eyes widening as we step out into a large hall.

It's stunning, the whole place glistens as if it were made out of a single block of black marble. Yet, as we move through the palace, I can't help but notice how barren it is. It's as if no one at all lives here.

I shake my head at this thought. Surely, that can't be right. This place is far too big for one person. He must at least have servants to help tend to it, right?

I peek up at him out of the corner of my eye. He towers over me, careful to keep his distance as we walk in silence. Suddenly, I find myself far more curious about him than the empty halls.

Are there really no others who live here? No wife, no friends to keep him company?

I chew my lip, curiosity burning bright within me, but my manners keep my questions from spilling out.

He has allowed me entry into his home, and I don't want to make him regret agreeing to our deal. I don't know if he can take it back now that it's been made, but I don't want to risk him sending me back to watch my father die simply because I asked too many questions. Besides, if the past few minutes are any indication, he seems to prefer silence.

So, I remain quiet, for now.

Our footsteps echo through the halls as we walk, his long strides forcing me to double my own pace. Still, I can't help peering into the rooms we pass, each one as bare as the last.

This palace of his must be even bigger than the king's castle in the capital. And yet, it's completely empty.

There are no nobles strolling through the halls, arm in arm as they gossip, or servants scurrying to tend to various tasks. No laughter, no music, no voices.

Nothing but the echo of our own steps.

Somehow, the quiet is even more unsettling than the swirling darkness that follows us, curling up the walls, around columns, and across every surface wherever we go. Finally, the silence grows to be too much for me.

"Your home is stunning, truly," I say, unable to keep my mouth shut any longer, "but it does seem awfully ... dead."

I cringe inwardly at my choice of words. I'd meant to say quiet, and quietly curse myself for the slip of my tongue.

My host snorts at this, but doesn't so much as glance my way, his eyes trained on the hall ahead.

My own mind races as I try to think of a way to fix things, before deciding that perhaps a joke will lighten the mood.

"I suppose, now that I'm here, I'll be able to breathe a little life into the place," I say, with a weak laugh.

"I like things the way they are."

"Oh, of course."

My cheeks burn with embarrassment as I realize that I've probably just offended him. Again. Sighing quietly, I try my best to push the feeling aside. It shouldn't matter much, not when I'll only be here for a few weeks before trading my life for Father's.

Turning, he leads me up a sweeping staircase and down another hall.

The longer we walk, the more I wonder if he means to tuck me away, locked in some room until our deal is complete. This thought has my stomach sinking with disappointment.

I steal one more glance up at him, taking in the stiffness

144

of his shoulders and the determination of his step.

He's dressed in all black, not an inch of his skin visible beneath the drape of the fabric, though it's impossible to deny the impressiveness of his form.

And then, there's the mask. It was obviously once the skull of some poor animal, but not one of any creature that I've ever seen.

What is he hiding beneath it?

Perhaps he's not a man at all, but a monster.

Not that it matters if he is. All that matters is that he is the one known as The Bargainer and that he keeps his side of the deal.

As far as I know, he's made of shadows, and I wouldn't be entirely surprised to learn there is no face beneath the mask. This thought has my brow knitting together, my imagination only growing wilder the more I try to quell it.

"This will be your room," he says, his voice startling me as it cuts through my thoughts and I nearly run straight into him.

Blinking, I realize that I was so distracted by my imagination that I hadn't noticed his steps slowing. Taking a nervous step back, I lean around him to look into the simple bed chamber beyond.

Like the rest of the palace, it's dark and cold; however, it isn't completely bare. Floor to ceiling curtains cover what I can only guess are windows on the far side of the room.

There's a large bed on one side of the room, as well as a lounge, wardrobe, and small table. Each piece is made of the same black material, all beautifully crafted. but missing a sense of, well, life.

An uncontrollable shiver races down my spine, and I quickly wrap my arms around myself in an effort to fight it off, but he's already noticed.

Without a word, he steps into the room, and I watch as he moves toward the fireplace.

He crouches, and I realize he means to light a fire for me. I step forward to assure him that I am no stranger to the task, but before I can even open my mouth, a fire is already roaring to life.

He flinches, stepping back from it as if burned by its heat.

"Thank you," I say, moving into the room, letting my eyes wander over everything before returning to him.

He simply watches me, and my cheeks flush with heat under his gaze. We say nothing to each other, and I shift nervously on my feet, curious if I should say something else. I'm not used to being a guest in someone else's house.

Captive or not.

Am I supposed to ask him for something? It seems rude, though I could certainly do with a bath and a fresh set of clothing.

Before I can decide whether or not to ask him for these things, he suddenly clears his throat.

"I will see you in the morning for breakfast," he says, nodding his head once before pivoting toward the door.

He's gone before I have a chance to respond, the door closing softly behind him as the last of his shadows slip beneath it.

I stare after him for a long moment before moving closer to the fire. Just like the one downstairs, the heat is subdued, but enough to fight off the chill that presses in around me.

I wonder what breakfast will be like in a place like this. My stomach growls at the thought, and I find myself comforted by my imagination as I picture all the possibilities.

Turning my back to the fire, I take a look around the room again before walking over to the heavy curtains and pulling one back. I'm greeted by a massive window as well as a rush of even icier air. I endure it long enough to peer out into the swirling mists beyond, but it's too dark to see whether we're still in the forest or somewhere else entirely.

Drawing the curtain again, I stifle a yawn as I turn my attention toward the bed. Slipping off my mud-caked shoes, I strip down to my underthings before pausing. The bottom hem of my chemise is muddied from my wandering, but I have nothing else to change into ... and in a strange place like this, I'd rather not get caught unawares and naked.

The bed is giant, unlike anything I've ever seen, though I suppose it would have to be to accommodate such towering creatures as my own host. I stare at it for a long moment, almost afraid to soil it with my dirty skin and clothes, but I ache to lie down.

It calls to me, inviting me in with its dark sheets and fluffy pillows. It suddenly dawns on me how silly it is to care about dirty sheets at a time like this. My time, what's left of it, shouldn't be wasted on such ridiculous worries.

Smiling to myself, I slip into the sheets, pulling them up to my chin as I let out a sigh of relief as the buttery silk welcomes me.

14

HAZEL

I wake with a groan, the very bones of my body aching with cold. Sitting up, I rub my eyes as I note that the fire has nearly died out.

For a long moment, I forget where I am, and I have to blink the last tendrils of sleep away before finally remembering.

Everything suddenly comes back in a cold rush that nearly steals my breath away. It hadn't been a dream after all.

Looking around the room, it's nearly pitch-black, save for a sliver of soft grey light filtering through a small gap in the curtains. I stare at it, surprised that there's any light here at all, considering the sheer weight of the shadows last night.

I stretch, eager to look out the window, only to nearly tumble off the lounge in the process. The bed had lasted all of two minutes, the chill permeating this place far too bitter to allow me to fall asleep so far from the fire. So, I'd stripped the sheets from the bed and then dragged the lounge as close to the flames as I dared.

Standing, I stretch again, my muscles stiff and more than a little sore. Grabbing the sheet, I wrap it around me before crossing to pull open the heavy curtains.

Light pools in, the obsidian-like marble almost seeming to drink it in. I let my eyes roam across the room once more. It feels like something about it has changed, though I can't put my finger on what is different about it.

The room is still barren and cold, but there's something otherworldly about the way the light pools and dances across the room. Almost as if daring the shadows to swallow it whole.

It's quite unlike anything I've ever seen before.

Turning back to the window, I step closer, pressing my nose to the glass to peer out into the strange world beyond.

But there's nothing to see. Nothing but mist and shadow and light.

My stomach growls, all too happy to remind me that it's been far too many hours since my last meal.

"Hush, now," I scold, pressing a hand to the ache now forming in my belly.

I return the sheets to the bed, before collecting my dirty dress from the floor. It's wrinkled and caked in mud, and I grimace as I pull it back on along with my socks and shoes.

I'll have to find a way to wash them, and soon.

Facing the door, I take a deep breath, squaring my shoulders as I try to accept the fact that I live here now, and I had better prepare myself for whatever that entails. At least, until our deal is fulfilled.

A chill settles into my bones once more, and I can't help wishing I had something warmer to wear. I step out into the empty hall, wrapping my arms around myself as another shiver racks my body.

As I walk, the whole place seems to echo around me, and the reality of my situation starts to set in.

I'm stuck here, in an empty palace a million miles away from home, caught between the shadows and entombed in a cold deeper than anything I've felt before.

I can't help but wonder if I can even call an existence here, however short, living. In a month's time, my life will come to an end, whether I like it or not.

My lip quivers at the thought, and it takes everything in me to push it away as I peer down yet another empty hallway.

Enough.

"Enough," I shout, stomping my foot once as my voice reverberates off the walls. "I refuse to live the rest of my days like this. I will not waste what remains of my life wallowing in self-pity. This is the fate I chose, and I am thankful for it. I made this choice, and I will stand by it. For Father's sake."

Satisfied with my own scolding, I set off once again to find my host, if not the kitchen first.

Of course, I'm not fool enough to think that the occasional dark thought won't rear its ugly head, but I refuse to let any more get the better of me.

The further I get from my room, the more the halls seem to echo around me. My eyes flit from room to room, and hall to empty hall, and I can't help but wonder just how amazing this place would be if just a little life was breathed into it.

A touch of warmth here and there to counter the icy loneliness that's settled within these walls.

I wonder who else has walked these halls, and whether this place, wherever it is, has always been like this. Part of me wonders if I even want to know the answers to these questions.

Wandering the halls, I get lost trying to find a way down to the lower floors where I'm sure the kitchen must be. It feels like I've been walking in circles by the time I finally make my way down, and then again have to work my way through another dark labyrinth of halls.

Eventually, I'm drawn to a large door by the clang of pots and pans being moved about. It sounds like someone has already begun cooking within, and I suddenly realize my heartbeat has quickened at the thought. I'm eager to meet whoever it is, and perhaps a bit too excited at the prospect of someone else being here.

I step toward the door but stop just short of bursting in.

I should knock. It sounds like whoever it is has their hands full, and I'm sure they wouldn't appreciate me being underfoot ... though I do hope they'll invite me in.

"Hello," I call out, knocking on the door loud enough to be heard above the din.

I'm greeted by a silence that stretches so long that I start to worry I was imagining the sounds from before.

"Wait in the dining room," comes the cold, deep voice of my host.

I hesitate for a moment, swallowing down my disappointment before doing as I've been told.

The dining room is just past the kitchen. As I step in, I can still hear the sound of far too many pots and pans banging together, as well as the low growl of an occasional curse that I'm almost certain I'm not meant to hear from what I can only assume is an adjoining door.

Fighting back a chuckle at the oddity of it all, I take a seat in one of the high-backed chairs surrounding the large dining table that looks like it could comfortably seat a small army. Looking around the cavernous room and all the empty chairs, I wonder yet again if this place was once full of life.

My thoughts are interrupted as the door at the far end of the room bursts open and the man from last night sweeps into the room. The shadows that ebb and flow around him seem to devour the light as he walks toward me, his arms laden with dishes.

He places the various dishes down on the table before me as well as a set of gold cutlery. Everything looks delicious, and my mouth waters as I take it all in. Tearing my eyes away from the food, I glance up to watch as my host moves to sit a few chairs away from me at the head of the table.

He's dressed more casually today in all black, the drape of his shirt falling open slightly to reveal a sliver of smooth marble-like skin as he leans forward in his chair. He's wearing a much simpler bone mask today, though it still covers the entirety of his face, but for the bottomless pools of his black eyes.

The small glimpse of skin I just saw has my curiosity piquing yet again at what lies beneath his mask.

"Eat," he says, waving at the food set before me.

I return my gaze to the food. As beautifully as it's been plated, none of it looks the least bit familiar, and I'm not entirely sure where to begin. Steam rises from one particularly strange-looking dish, the scent pungent but inviting. Reaching for the fork, my stomach growls, eager to be filled.

Pausing, I glance back at my host, realizing he hasn't set a place for himself or moved to join me. Instead, watching me intently from the head of the table.

"Will you be joining me?"

"No, I had my fill last night," he says with a shake of his head. "Besides, I do not require food the same way you mortals do."

His words cause wariness to wash over me at the way he says this, and I can't help but wonder what exactly he is. Giving him a small smile, I turn back to the food and reach out to stick a fork in the steaming plate closest to me.

My stomach lets out an embarrassing growl as I bring the food to my lips. Taking a tentative bite, I freeze, the fork still in my mouth. A foul, bitter flavor fills my mouth as my eyes water. My stomach clenches as I try desperately not to gag.

Just barely, I manage to swallow the bite, praying to the gods that it doesn't kill me later. It's a struggle to maintain my composure as I set my fork down. Fighting to keep my face from revealing the horror of what I've just experienced, my eyes flicker to him, but it's too late.

He's leaning sideways in his chair, his elbow propped against the armrest as his finger presses to the forehead of his mask.

"It is awful, is it not?" he sighs deeply. "My apologies. I do not know what I did wrong. No matter how hard I tried, no matter how perfectly I plated them, they all tasted wrong. I had hoped it was merely a matter of human taste. Clearly, I was wrong."

I open my mouth to reply, but he's already gotten to his feet and moved to clear the plates from the table. The shadows whirling wildly about him, icy chills shooting through my body every time they graze against me, as if revealing the depth of his own frustration.

I watch him, worrying my bottom lip between my teeth as I wonder if I should say something.

Straightening, he nods once to me before retreating from the room, his arms full of the barely edible food.

I watch after him, the door just barely closing behind him before I leap to my feet to chase after him.

Without bothering to knock this time, I push my way into the kitchen behind him, only to stop abruptly as I glance about the room.

I've walked straight into pure chaos, it would seem.

Pots and pans are piled in haphazard towers, flour and batter coat nearly every surface, and dirty plates are strewn about the floor. He would have had to have been toiling in here for hours to make this kind of mess, if not all night.

His back is to me as I take a deep breath and cautiously move further into the kitchen. I run my hand over a copper pan and then peer into the pantry. It's stocked full of ingredients that I could have only dreamed of having before.

"Perhaps you might allow me to make us something this morning?" I ask, turning away from the pantry. "It seems only fair after all that I find some way to repay you for opening your home to me."

"No."

My heart sinks slightly at his refusal.

"I'm an excellent cook," I try again. "My mother taught me before she fell ill, and I've enjoyed it ever since."

"No," he says again, his voice sharper. "It is my job as your host."

"Be that as it may, I would like the chance to familiarize myself with this place, if I'm to live here. Besides, I'm telling you that I want to cook," I say, frowning at his back, before adding, "I am your guest after all, am I not?"

He slowly turns toward me, and I wish I could see his face. That I could read whatever emotions are flickering across it as he watches me. Through the holes in his mask, his onyx eyes remain cold and unnerving as they stare into my very depths. But as the shadows rise and fall around him, settling into calm waves at his feet, I get the sense that I shouldn't rely on his eyes to tell me what he's thinking.

"Very well," he says with a sigh, gesturing toward the surrounding mess. "The kitchen is yours."

I give him a bright smile.

"Thank you, now, go sit over there," I say, pointing to a stool in the far corner of the room, before quickly turning back to the pantry before he can see the widening of my eyes. I hurry to make myself busy, hardly believing I just told him what to do in his own house.

Grabbing several large brown eggs from a shelf, I reach to pluck from the drying herbs above, smiling as their earthy fragrance colors the air around me.

Satisfied with my selection, I step from the pantry with a smile on my face. I pretend not to notice that he's perched on the stool I'd pointed to, but I can feel his eyes on me as I work.

Weaving my way through the mess he created, I do my best to tidy as I go. I've never been in a kitchen this well-stocked, let alone so sophisticated, and I rather enjoy the process of familiarizing myself with everything.

Setting the copper pan on the stove, I crack the eggs into it before turning to collect an odd assortment of dishes and placing them in the sink while I wait.

His eyes never leave me as I move about his kitchen, humming softly under my breath to keep my nerves at bay.

It isn't long before some order has been restored, and I can breathe a little easier. Once the eggs begin to sizzle, the smell of herbs filling the kitchen, my shoulders finally relax.

Plating the eggs, I take a deep breath before walking toward my host.

"Here," I say, setting one plate in front of him. "Try this."

I perch on a stool next to him as I turn to face him, balancing my own plate on my knees. It's unladylike, I know, and I'm sure Merelda would have a half dozen choice words for me if she could see me now, but I don't care.

Tasting my own eggs, I savor the bite before peeking up

at him. He's staring down at his own plate as if unsure whether or not to trust it. Slowly, he reaches for the fork, and I have to bite back a chuckle as he warily pokes at the food.

He's hesitant as he picks some of the egg up with his fork, and I realize I've stopped eating to watch. My eyes are glued to the fork as it makes its way toward his face.

For one thrilling moment, I think he's about to remove his mask, but he simply turns and slips the fork beneath it.

"Hmm."

"I know it's simple food," I start just as his dark eyes meet mine and I find myself lost for words. As he chews, I almost swear I see his eyes brighten and the shadows clinging to him sway, as if dancing. I feel my cheeks flood with warmth at the thought and quickly drop my gaze back to my plate.

"This is by far the best thing I have tasted in ... Well, since I came to reside here. Perhaps even before then."

His words have the heat in my cheeks flaming out to fill my entire body. For the first time since I arrived here, I feel warm.

I don't remember the last time someone complimented my meal, aside from Father. Blinking back tears as I stare down at my own food, I struggle to find a way to stop them. To distract myself, I muster what little courage he's suddenly sparked in me to ask a question.

"Where is here, exactly?"

"The in-between."

Color me intrigued as the tears all but disappear at his answer.

"What?" I ask, glancing up at him.

"This place, my home, is the in-between. The realm that lies between the living and the dead, the mortals and the immortals, everything that is, was, or ever will be," he explains. "It is the stitching that holds the universe together."

"Oh."

"You are right to look confused. It is not a place commonly thought of, let alone spoken of. Most dare not believe it even exists."

"Then, how is it that we are here?" I ask. "Talking and eating as one might in the world of the living?"

He's quiet for a long moment as if contemplating whether or not to answer.

"I am the sole guardian of this place," he finally says. "Only I am allowed to grant entrance or leave from this place. It is through me that we can sit here as we would in your own home."

I consider this for a moment.

"The food, is it real?" I ask, the question slipping from my lips before I've even had a chance to think it.

There's a second of surprised silence between us before he chuckles deeply.

"Yes, the food is from your own realm. You need not worry about that."

Peering up at him through my lashes, I suddenly realize that I don't know what his real name is. The name the witch, Ravynn, gave me doesn't quite seem to suit him. The Bargainer seems like an odd way to address him, but I can't very well continue to live here simply thinking of him as the man.

They were both clear that he was a being known by many names, after all.

"What name are you best known by in my own realm?" I ask quietly. "Before I met Ravynn, I'd never heard of anyone by the name of The Bargainer, and, if you'll forgive me for saying so, it doesn't quite seem to suit you."

His eyes search my face as he sets down his plate.

"No, very few people have known me by that name, and never one such as yourself," he answers.

"Then what name should I know you by?" I ask.

"I am the one they call Death."

15

DEATH

I can see that my answer has startled the girl.

Her face has paled, her large blue eyes wide as they blink up at me. Everything about her has suddenly cooled and dimmed as fear wraps its tendrils around her, and I feel the heavy weight of disappointment settle over me as I watch her.

Normally, this very reaction would delight me as I watched mere mortals consider what my very presence meant for them. Fear feeding me pieces of their souls as it tore into them like the beast that it was.

Yet, seeing her eyes grow dim as I feel fear claw at her soul, does little to bring me joy. In fact, I feel horrified with myself. I mean the girl no harm, as long as she is a guest in my home, however temporary that may be. And yet, I have done just that with my answer.

Still, I do not know why I feel so displeased by her reaction. What should I care what a mortal thinks of me when she is just that.

Mortal.

Perhaps it is because she is the only mortal to ever step foot in my home, and likely the last. Or perhaps, it is because so few mortals ever look upon me.

They know when I am coming for them. They can feel my presence in their final moments, but they do not know me but for a brief moment.

Her presence here is as strange to me as I am undoubtedly to her. It suddenly strikes me that I am becoming sentimental toward her.

Her. A creature of such insignificance. She is but a fleeting moment in the great expanse of time, despite what the Fates may say otherwise.

With a deep sigh, I push my feelings aside, allowing indifference to fill its place.

It should be a relief that she will be the last and only mortal to step foot here. My palace, my realm, would not survive the test of time if there were others.

Especially, if they were all like her. Her cheerful optimism in the face of certain death ... it throws off the entire atmosphere of my sanctuary.

Death is a cold, cruel thing. I should know.

I *am* Death.

I have spent my entire existence embracing it. I have cloaked myself in darkness, forgotten what warmth feels like.

And yet here she is, bringing the very thing into my home.

Should my palace not be a true reflection of myself? I do not know how to process the way her sunlight

161

seems to melt away the very shadows that make up my being.

It does not matter. I will not have to endure it for long.

She is mortal, after all, and we have a deal. Nothing more, nothing less, exists between us.

One month of sunshine will do little to thaw an eternity of darkness.

I am simply playing the part of a good host. It is my job to keep watch over her soul, until our deal is complete.

That is all.

"You need not fear me," I say, rising from the stool. "Not yet, not before your time has come. Now, if you will excuse me, I have business to attend to."

She does not say anything, my presence clearly unsettling her.

As it should.

"My name is Hazel," the girl whispers, giving me pause. I had not expected to hear her voice again so soon.

Not knowing how else to react, I simply nod once to excuse myself and turn toward the kitchen door. If I am to watch over her soul until the next moonless night, it seems I will have to make myself scarce. I will not have her living in constant fear of me until then.

My brow knits together at this, surprised by the strength of my desire for her to be comfortable here.

"Please, what am I to do all day?" the girl asks, her voice quiet.

I turn to look at her, finding her eyes wide and uncertain as she looks at me. I frown, wondering why she would feel the need to ask me this. Do mortals now require a keeper for the structure of their days as well?

I consider her question for a long moment, before finally deciding on an answer.

"What is it that you would like to do with your time here?"

Her mouth opens, but no words find their way past her lips. She blinks, her brow furrowing as she closes her mouth again. She looks almost as confounded by my question as I was hers.

How strange.

Then, too late, I realize her eyes have become drowned in unshed tears as she lifts them to meet mind.

"What is wrong?" I demand, worry making my voice sharper than I had intended, making me wince as she flinches.

"No, nothing is wrong," she says.

"Then why are your eyes wet?"

She gives me a shaky smile as she quickly lifts her hand to wipe away the tears.

"It's just that I can't seem to remember the last time that I was given a choice."

Rage unfurls within my chest, burning through me at her response. Without giving myself time to pause and consider, I allow it to drive my response. Closing the distance between us, I lean down reaching one gloved hand to lift her chin toward me as I look her in the eye.

"As long as you are a guest in my home, little creature, your time is yours to do with what you please. Do whatever it is that brings you pleasure, or simply spend them doing nothing at all," I say, my voice as gentle as I can make it. "Unless the Fates, or I, have great need for you, then you are free to spend your days here with me as you please, understood?"

She gives me a small nod, and I drop my hand as I straighten.

"Good. Now, tell me, what is it that you would like to fill your days with?"

She tilts her head slightly in thought before meeting my gaze again, my own having tilted to match hers as I realize I am curious to hear what she says. A small smile tugs at her lips, and I find my attention drawn to them for a breath.

"Paint," she answers, the word soft and nearly breathless. "I would like to spend my days painting."

"Hmm."

I consider this for a moment, then I give her a nod and take a step back. It was hard to ignore how her breaths had become shallow as I drew near, or the way she struggled not to recoil at my touch.

Or how much I disliked that she did, but now is not the time to care about such trivial things. Not when I have paints and canvas to get for her.

"I will see what I can do," I say, stopping short of speaking her name, before once more turning to leave the kitchen, and her, behind.

16

HAZEL

Death sweeps from the room as I wipe the back of my sleeve across my eyes once again.

A wave of guilt washes over me at the fear I'd felt toward him after learning the name we humans use for him. Again, I can't help but feel like it doesn't suit him.

Not truly.

Death may be what he is, but I don't think it's who he is.

This place, his home, may be built of shadows and ice, but he is not, despite what he may think. There's a warmth to him, buried deep within his eyes, as he watches me.

No, Death does not suit him. I'll have to think of another name to call him by while I'm here, even if it's just within my own mind.

Sighing, I realize I'm not making much sense, but how can I? The man is literally death personified.

My mind swims, and I shake my head to clear it. I need something to keep my hands and thoughts occupied.

Climbing off the stool, I turn to survey the kitchen.

Much of the mess remains, and I smile. At least I know what to do with myself for now. This thought is a welcome one, and I'm grateful for the distraction.

I'd almost been afraid of the empty halls earlier. Afraid that with nothing to keep me busy, I'd spend my days wandering them in silence as I wallowed over the choice that I've made ... on the heartbreak and disappointment Father will know when he learns of my fate.

If he learns my fate at all.

My mind momentarily flits back to Cyprian standing over Amadeus' body, and I grow sick at the thought of what lies may be told to Father about me.

No, I cannot focus on that now.

Not when there's a kitchen in desperate need of attention. Turning toward it, I busy my hands. It soon becomes clear that it's been ages since the place was last organized. Perhaps even longer since it was last properly cleaned.

It seems even this realm struggles with the most humble aspects of our universe, as Death had called it.

Dust has collected on nearly every surface, hardened into grime around the sink and corners of the countertops. Rolling up my sleeves, I welcome the challenge as I set to work.

Finding a rather long apron forgotten in a back corner of the pantry, I have to roll it several times before tying it around my waist. I can't imagine it belonging to Death, and yet, I can't quite picture who he'd have working in his kitchen ... or why they aren't here anymore.

Scrubbing the pantry, I come across three perfectly round golden potatoes and two long carrots, as well as an assortment of delicious smelling herbs and spices. Smiling, I decide to start a stew for dinner while I clean.

It isn't long before the kitchen is warm with the savory aroma of vegetables and herbs. I sing as I tidy up the pots and pans, not caring that my fingers have begun to wrinkle, or that my arms have grown sore from scrubbing.

All too soon, though, the kitchen is spotless, the pantry organized, and the stew happily simmering away over the fire. Aside from waiting, there's not much else for me to do.

Sighing, I take off my apron, putting it away before moving toward the door. I'm just about to leave when I realize I need a way to easily find my way back.

I hurry over to the pantry, carefully picking out one of the jars of spices. Sniffing it, I wrinkle my nose at it before sneezing.

Hopefully, Death will forgive me for this.

It hasn't been more than a few hours since I first stepped into the kitchen, and I'm not entirely sure what I'm supposed to do with myself now. Other than roam the halls, hoping that I don't trespass and upset my host.

Outside of the kitchen, everything is as spotless as it is cold and lifeless ... until I begin sprinkling the spice's fine powder along one edge of the hall that is. I wonder how he manages to keep it so clean, especially after what I just dealt with in the kitchen.

Moving from room to room, I peer in at them. Most are empty, as expected, but a few have random assortments of black and gold furniture. One sitting room in particular calls to me, a large ornate armchair with fluffy gold pillows sits atop a thick rug, the shelves lining the walls filled to the brim with thick books.

But my excitement is soon quelled as I pull one of the books off the shelf, the sheer weight of it nearly impossible for me to hold. Laying it down on the rug, I flip it open only to realize it's written in a language I've never seen before.

Of course.

After a great deal of struggle, I manage to return the book to its shelf before continuing on.

It doesn't take long for me to realize that Death has impeccable taste when it comes to furnishings, even if everything is dark and cold. There's not an ounce of color or warmth to be found within these walls.

Aside from the kitchen, and even that seems out of place here. The only room in this sprawling palace where there's any sign that someone might actually live here. That this isn't simply a mausoleum for Death and his untouched possessions.

I frown at this thought as I move on to yet another sitting room. Everything here is otherworldly in its somber beauty, but it all just feels so empty.

So forlorn.

There are no people, no voices or laughter, to chase away the shadows that lurk in every corner. Always there, but just out of sight.

Even the rooms that have pieces of furniture don't seem to hold any life or purpose.

My wandering leads me to a towering set of black doors within a cavernous entryway. I stop just short of them, realizing that just beyond them lie the misty grounds of this realm.

Am I allowed to walk them? Do I even dare test the limits of my welcome here by venturing outside without permission?

I place my hand on the golden handle just above my head before thinking twice.

It's not worth the risk of trying.

Dropping my hand, I turn and walk toward a sweeping set of stairs that I can only hope will eventually lead me back to my room.

The next two days slip past in much the same manner.

Only Death seems to be nowhere to be found, and the halls seem emptier than ever ... aside from the little trails of different colored spices that I now use to guide me through them.

I'd half expected to come across him in the halls or to share our meals together, but no. As far as I can tell, I'm utterly alone in this cavernous place.

My meals are quiet affairs as I eat next to the fire in the kitchen, the one room I've felt drawn to over the past couple days. Though, I suppose that's in part because it's the only room with anything for me to do.

I fill my time with chopping, mixing, and tasting, the countertops now laden with cakes, breads, and various dishes. It's exciting having so many ingredients to work with, many of which I've only ever read about, but with each new dish, my heart aches a little more.

After all, what's the point when there's no one to share them with?

Time seems to stretch and pull at me as the hours slip past. I try my best to busy myself, to distract my mind from this strange reality I've found myself in, but there is little else to do but wait.

On the morning of the third day, I wake with a start. Frowning up at the dark ceiling of my room, I take a deep breath as I try to calm my racing heart.

A chill creeps over my skin as I realize something must have woken me, and then I feel it.

Or rather, *him*.

Sitting up, it takes less than a minute for my eyes to search him out in the far corner of my room. Standing, nearly entirely shrouded in swirling shadows aside from his bone mask, stands Death.

"Ah, you are awake," he says, his eyes brightening behind the mask.

"Of course, I'm awake," I say, "you frightened me half to ..."

I trail off, realizing what I was about to say.

"To what?" he asks, the darkness curling up around him as he cocks his head to one side.

I pause, my cheeks flushing before I answer quietly, "Death."

There's a quiet moment of silence before a deep laugh spills from him to fill the room. He blinks, and I can't help but smile at how his eyes widen at the sound, or the way his laugh felt wrapping around me.

Clearing his throat, Death takes a moment to compose himself before he steps closer.

"Come, I have something to show you, now that you are awake."

He strides over to the door, as I extract myself from the nest of pillows and blankets that I've made on the floor by the fire. My back to him, I'm careful to wrap one of the sheets around me, the thin chemise I've been sleeping in hardly enough to hide my modesty.

I glance over my shoulder to realize he's still watching, as he holds open the door for me.

"I-I need to dress," I say, my cheeks burning even hotter.

His eyes drop to take me in before he quickly drags them away, his posture stiffening as if he's just realized what he's done.

"Of course," he says quickly. "I will wait for you in the hall."

The moment the door closes behind him, I scurry to pull on my dress. It's clean, though still a little damp from washing it the day before.

I grimace as the dampness of the fabric deepens the chill of this place, and pray he won't notice the untidiness of the now-wrinkled fabric. Finished dressing, I step out into the hall where Death motions for me to follow him.

We walk in silence, his shadows swirling excitedly around my ankles, occasionally drifting high enough to brush frostily over my skin. I glance up at Death just as his eyes flicker away from me. Watching him more closely, I get the sense that there's a question on his mind that he's trying to decide how to ask.

"Is something wrong?" I ask, worried that he'll never ask if I don't say something first.

"The bed," he says, as if relieved I've asked. "Is it not to your liking?"

My cheeks burn yet again at his question, and I struggle to find the words to answer him.

"Why did I find you asleep on the floor, little one?" he presses. "If the bed is unsatisfactory, I can find a new one for you. All you must do is ask."

"It's not the bed," I say, my voice quiet as I train my eyes on the marble floor.

"Then what is it?"

"It's ... it's just too cold. I sleep better with the warmth of the fire to comfort me."

He's quiet for a long moment before he mutters something under his breath that I can't quite make out. Though the anger in his voice is clear enough to give me pause as I peek up at him through my lashes.

He lets out a deep sigh, his dark eyes shifting to me briefly before he looks away again.

"I promise I will do something about that, at once," he says.

"It's really not—"

"I will not have you sleeping on the floor of my own home," he growls, cutting me off.

I swallow, my heart beating in my chest from the ferocity in his voice, unsure how to respond. His steps slow until we're left standing in the middle of the hallway, glancing at each other, but not fully meeting one another's gaze.

Embarrassment and shame mix within me as I realize that, yet again, I've found a way to offend him.

"I—"

"Thank you," I say, accidentally cutting him off and triggering another stretch of silence between us. Another grumble of displeasure rolls from him, and unable to help myself, I glance up at him. His eyes don't meet mine as they move over my body instead, causing heat to burn brighter within me.

"Your outfit," he says. "Forgive me, I should have realized sooner that you would require new clothing. I will see to it that you get some."

"Please," I start, my voice barely a whisper, "you needn't go through all this trouble for me. I've made do with far less and for far longer. You've already provided me with so much."

"Enough," he tells me, anger flashing in his eyes. "Your days of want are over, little one. You will want for nothing as long as you remain under my roof. Now, tell me, is there anything else you need?"

I have to bite back my refusal of his kindness, fearing that it will only make him more upset. He watches me intently, and I find myself unable to bear the intensity of his gaze.

"I-I don't think so," I answer.

Finally, with a sigh, he nods down the hall, and we continue on in silence. I trail a few steps behind him, risking small glances his way. I'm not quite sure what to think of his reaction, or how quick he seems to anger.

Suddenly stopping before a closed door, Death glances down at me.

"This," he says, opening the door for me, "is to be your studio."

I stare up at him in disbelief before stepping into the room. I inhale sharply as I take in the quality of the easels, pigments, oils, brushes, and everything in between. It's better than anything I could have imagined.

"Is it pleasing to you?"

"Yes," I breathe, moving deeper into the room. "I love it."

Running a hand over a collection of canvas, I turn to give him a smile, my heart full as I meet his gaze.

"Good. Remember, should you want for anything, you need only ask."

This is the kindest and most extravagant thing anyone has ever done for me. I don't know how I will ever be able to repay him for this, but I will try.

From the doorway, he watches me, his dark eyes shining just as bright as my own, and I suddenly understand his earlier reaction.

He wasn't angry with me, but with himself. I suppose I would be too, if I knew I could provide someone with such joy and comfort but failing to do so.

"Thank you."

He nods once, his hand still on the door handle, and I realize he's about to leave.

Without a moment's hesitation, I hurry toward him. He takes a step back, pulling back, but he's not quick enough.

My arms wrap around him as I bury my face against his hard chest. He tenses, his arms held up on either side of me in surprise.

He smells fresh, like a forest after snowfall, and I allow myself to quietly breathe him in for a moment. Realizing I probably smell far worse after days of just rinsing myself off in the sink, I quickly step back.

Tears wet my cheeks as I glance up at him.

"What is wrong?" he asks, his eyes flashing with concern as the shadows around him seem to darken.

I laugh this time, shaking my head as I brush the tears from my cheeks.

"Nothing," I assure him. "Quite the opposite, actually. I'm just so grateful for everything you've done for me."

His head cocks to the side as he watches me, and I smile up at him, knowing I look a right mess but not caring. Death lets out a small sigh, shaking his head at me.

"You humans are such strange creatures," he mutters, pulling another small laugh from me. "Is there anything else I can do for you before I leave?"

I hesitate for a second before answering, "If possible, I'd like to bathe at some point—"

"Consider it done. Now, little one, go paint to your heart's content." I don't hesitate to obey as I start to turn away from him, but he grabs my arm. I blush, hoping he can't smell me as he holds me in place and leans forward. "And about your dress ..."

"What about it?" I ask, looking up at him.

"Burn it," he says, his eyes moving lower as he growls low against my ear. "Burn it all."

With that, he releases me. I take a step back, blinking in surprise, the space where he stood only a second ago now empty. As if he was never there at all.

I stare at the empty space a moment longer before turning back to face the room, and the paints and canvases that sing my name.

17

DEATH

I press a hand to the ache in my chest, frowning down at myself as I lean against the wall just outside the studio.

What is this strange feeling?

The way she touched me just a moment ago ... I felt something within me shift.

I do not remember the last time another chose to touch me. As painful as the heat of her was, there was something in the way she threw her arms around me that made me want her to do it again.

Perhaps this is just what comes of spending time with a living soul. I have always heard there were terrible consequences to interacting directly with mortals.

Until her, I have never had to worry about what those consequences might be. I have never had to worry about the effect a mortal might have on me.

Seeing her smile, her joy over the simplest things, makes me want to bend the world to kneel at her feet.

It is a struggle to remind myself that she is temporary.

As with nearly everything I have ever known, her time here is not permanent. Too soon, she will be but a distant memory. Her life, her very presence in my home, is fleeting.

These feelings, this *warmth*, cannot last.

Too soon, I will have to claim her soul for its final journey.

Pushing away from the wall, I storm through my palace, the darkness rising up to meet me as I shut myself away in my room.

Locking the door, I reach up to pry off my mask.

Running a hand over my face, I get a glimpse of my reflection out of the corner of my eye. I cross the room, bracing myself against the counter as I lean over it to stare at the man in the mirror.

He stares back at me, the cruelty in his eyes unmistakable.

Disgust rolls off of me in waves as I slam my fist down on the counter and turn my back to the mirror, unable to look upon my reflection a moment longer.

How could I ever hope that she might see me as anything other than a monster?

What right do I have to want her to?

I am no fool. Try as I might to deny it, I know what these feelings mean for me ... but for her, they would only lead to death.

Guilt weighs heavily on me. I should know better than to want what I cannot have, and yet, I also know that I am selfish.

If I am not careful, I will call her soul home before its time.

Drawing myself up, I inhale deeply, slowly exhaling as I check my emotions.

I have no choice but to force my heart to stop thawing. It must harden itself against these feelings.

Against *her*.

Despite how hard it is to ignore the pang of bitter sadness and regret, I remind myself that this is the only way.

I know better than to tempt the Fates and what has been decided for me.

There is no warmth, no happiness for a monster such as me, and I would do well to remember that.

Closing my eyes, I allow myself to draw strength from the darkness, allowing the cold bitterness of life to fill me. Finally satisfied that I have drowned any more of my foolish thoughts of warmth and love within me, I move toward my wardrobe.

The day is young, and there is much work to be done. Removing my outer layer, I pause as my hand catches on something in the pocket.

Pulling it out, I turn over the small book in the palm of my hand. I had meant to return it to the girl earlier, but the thought had slipped my mind.

Placing it down on a table, I finish changing. My outfit drapes well over my form, heavy chains weighing it down in a display of strength and power.

Selecting a new mask, I let out a sigh before placing it over my face. Now hidden behind a mask, I turn to adjust the final details of my outfit in the mirror, but in doing so, my eyes keep flickering to the book in its reflection.

With a low growl of frustration, I finish pulling on a new pair of leather gloves and reach for it. I stare down at the tiny book for a long moment, contemplating whether or not to leave it here, before finally tucking it inside my pocket.

I will deal with it later.

For now, I must return to the mortal realm.

18

HAZEL

The next few days pass in an artistic daze.

I spend just about every minute in my studio, only leaving to grab several of the dishes I'd prepared in the kitchen, and a few blankets.

With Death yet again nowhere to be found, I find myself curling up to sleep in the room, unwilling to leave behind the precious gift he gave me. The second I open my eyes, I'm happily back at the easel painting as I munch on a handful of cake or bread.

Finally, I step back to admire the piece that's kept me in its hold the past few days.

It's perfect.

A smile tugs at the corner of my mouth as I clasp my hands together in excitement. Tidying up the studio, I decide that I can't wait for Death to come to me. Wiping my hands on my skirts, I open the door and leave the studio behind in search for him.

Turning a corner, I catch a glimpse of my reflection in

the shine of the walls and whirl on it. Tentatively, I step forward to get a better look. Dried paint is smeared across my face and dress, my hair matted in some places and sticking out wildly in others.

Change of plans. It seems that I am in desperate need of a bath, first.

With one last horrified look at myself, I turn and head back toward my bedroom, thankful to find my spice trails have yet to disappear. I'm almost shocked Death hasn't mentioned them.

Thankful that I don't run into Death along the way, given the state I'm in, I quickly open the door to my room and shut it tightly behind me. Leaning against the door, I glance around, worried for a moment that I've entered the wrong room.

But that's simply not the case.

Given the way every other room in the house looks, there's no way Death would ever decorate a room like this, unless absolutely necessary.

The furniture has all been rearranged, the bed pushed as close to the fire as is safe to allow, and a heavy canopy added to the other three sides. Heavy rugs now cover the floor and thick furs blanket the bed.

Even the fire somehow seems to burn brighter and hotter. There's even a large copper tub already filled with water beside it, complete with a tray of soaps, oils, and powders.

Turning, I find the wardrobe open, and my heart nearly stops in my chest. Hanging within it are more dresses than I've ever seen at once.

Stepping closer, I run my hand over them as I take in the heavy velvets, wools, and silks, each delicately embroidered or otherwise intricately designed. They're stunning. Many of them are made in a fashion I've never seen before, let alone wore, but all of the dresses match Death's impeccable taste.

Delicate undergarments have been neatly folded to one side, as well as fresh socks and small items.

There's even a pair of slippers as well as new boots and a fur-lined cloak.

A wave of guilt crashes over me as I realize I have no idea how long his generosity has gone unnoticed. I must thank him as soon as possible for this.

I should have returned to my room sooner; he must think me so ungrateful.

How long have these dresses been here waiting for me?

I cross the room to dip my hand in the water.

Tepid, and only thanks to the fire, I'm sure.

It's probably been a day, if not longer, since he brought these things here for me. No wonder I haven't seen him.

Well, I can't allow him to think the worst of me any longer. I must set things right immediately.

I don't know why the thought of him thinking poorly of me upsets me so much, but I don't allow myself to mull over the feeling. Instead, I hurry to strip out of my clothes and step into the bath.

I refuse to allow my shivering to keep me from thoroughly washing my hair and body, scrubbing hard to rid myself of paint, dirt, and oil. By the time I'm finally satisfied with my cleanliness, my skin is pink and floral scented.

I don't think I've ever felt this fresh, or smelled this beautiful.

Drying myself with a thick towel, I select one of the dresses at random from the wardrobe, determined to wear as many of them as I can before ...

Well, before it's too late.

Pushing this thought from my mind, I lay the garment across the bed. Admiring it, I braid my hair loosely before carefully pulling the dress on.

Stepping toward the shiniest part of the wall, I spin slowly to get a good look at myself.

Light moves over the heavy silk like a dark waterfall, the waist structured perfectly to give my bust support while accentuating all my femininity in the most elegant way.

The sleeves leave my shoulders bare as they drape down over my arms instead. The neckline is nearly as deep as the dress Merelda gave me, but somehow, it makes me look regal rather than exposed.

Though the scar from Lord Payne's ring is now visible.

It almost makes me happy to see it, happy to know he's probably seething somewhere at the news of my disappearance.

I start to reach for the slippers, but pause, choosing the new pair of boots instead. After all, it could take me all day to track Death down to thank him. They fit perfectly, and I can't help wondering how he managed to get my measurements so perfect.

It seems Death has more than kept his word, and now, I intend to keep mine.

Collecting my old things from the floor, I stand next to

the fire for a moment, holding on to these last remnants of my past life. Stepping closer, I pause, my mind suddenly racing back to those final moments with Cyprian.

The book.

I rummage through my things, but find nothing, realizing I'd washed the dress a few days ago and it hadn't seen it then either.

My stomach twists.

Could I have lost it in the forest?

My heart sinks as I come to terms with this being the most likely situation. Still, perhaps I should mention it to Death. It's possible he's seen it, or—as terrible as I feel even thinking to ask it of him—can rescue it from the forest for me.

This eases my mind, and I push my worry over the book aside for the time being.

Reaching for the cloak, I lay it over my shoulders, thrilled to find it just as warm as it is beautiful. Smiling at my reflection, I finally step out of my room in search of Death.

The clip of my new boots fills the halls as I walk, almost giving me the impression that I'm not entirely alone here.

I feel like a princess as I walk through the palace, my skirts sweeping behind me. Everything that he has given me is far more luxurious and expensive than I had ever expected, and I can't help feeling guilty. Guilty that I won't be able to make much use out of them for long, and guiltier still that I haven't thanked him sooner.

I can only hope that I haven't offended him.

It doesn't take long for me to realize Death is nowhere

to be found. I search every empty room I can find, but even his shadows have left no trace of him.

Frowning, I realize I have no other choice but to wait for his return. I will not let another moment pass between us without me showing him my gratitude.

Making my way downstairs, I find myself drawn to the main room where he first brought me. A large fire roars in the fireplace, beckoning me closer with its warmth.

Glancing over to one dark corner, I pause, frowning at a pile of strange fabric within. Walking over to it, I crouch to get a better look at it, turning it over in my hand. It's black, and made entirely out of feathers, but something about it feels disturbingly familiar.

Only when my hand grazes against a metal clasp do I realize why. This is the cloak the witch gave me, but it looks nothing like it now. Gone is the soft pink garment that had done so little to keep me warm in those final moments in the forest.

I suppose it was probably enchanted. I snort at the thought.

It wasn't long ago that I'd been teasing Cyprian about wanting to see a magician, and now, here I was in the middle of *real* magic. The thought of Cyprian has the little book springing to mind again, and I quickly search the cloak for it.

Nothing.

Sighing, I rise and settle onto the lounge, my hands folded in my lap as I stare absentmindedly into the fire. Surely, he won't be too long.

At least, I hope not.

I can hardly wait to not only thank him for his overwhelming kindness toward me, but to show him the results of the gifts he's given me.

All too slowly, the minutes drag into hours, and I find myself shifting in my spot. Eventually, I draw my legs up onto the seat, leaning to one side as I try to make myself more comfortable.

My fingers itch to be back in my studio, but I don't give in.

When Death does come home, I know that I'll be able to hear his footsteps from in here. That alone is enough to keep me where I am. Still, I soon find myself fighting the urge to close my eyes.

I want to be awake when he returns. But it's a losing battle, and soon I find myself giving in to the coziness of my new clothes, and the warmth of the fire, as I close my eyes.

I find myself wading through a thick fog, darkness licking out in tendrils around my feet, driving me ever forward. Suddenly, I step out of the fog and find myself standing in front of my home.

Frowning, I shiver as a prickling sensation races across my skin and turn my head to find Death pushing his way through the front door.

I stare after him for a moment, my heart skipping a beat in my chest as the blood runs cold in my veins.

There could only be one reason why he's here.

Father.

I try to scream, but nothing comes out. I feel like I'm drowning in sorrow and no one can hear me as I run toward the door.

Throwing it open, I suddenly find myself in a tavern. Cyprian sits at a table in the back corner, drowning his sorrows in one mug of ale after another. He only rises once to throw a punch at someone who dares to jeer at him.

I try to push through the crowd to get to him, but it's impossible. Tears sting my eyes as I see the pain in his own. His features sharper with sorrow.

I hate to think that I have caused this pain. That now his suffering is greater because of me.

Again, I try to call out, but no sound escapes me.

Suddenly, his eyes shift to mine, and for a moment, I think he can see me ... but then he turns, calling out for another ale before leaning forward against the table.

Again, a chill creeps over my skin, and I turn to find Death watching him from the dark corner of the room.

I blink as I start to move toward him, only to find myself back at home. Merelda stands before me, her hair a mess and her cheeks stained with tears.

It takes me a moment to realize we're both standing in her private room, where she readied me to meet Lord Payne. I stare at her as she grabs a cracked basin and sends it flying into the wall across the room.

It shatters into a thousand pieces as her crying turns to manic laughter as she screams curses at my name. Stepping back, my eyes never leaving her, my hands are quick to find the doorknob, but the door is jammed.

Whirling on it, I throw my body against it. I stumble

forward only to find myself in my father's room. Blinking at the empty bed, my eyes lift to find Father standing by the window.

There's a book in his hand, tears staining his cheeks as he stares out at the empty sky.

Again, I try to call to him, but he doesn't so much as glance over his shoulder. My words disappearing into the shadows that suddenly swirl up to wrap themselves around me, holding me back as I glance up to find Death standing beside me.

His eyes trained on Father.

He moves past me, as I silently scream for him to stop. I watch as he reaches out to place a hand on my father's shoulder, the book falling from his hand as he slowly drops to his knees before Death.

No!

This can't be happening. It's too soon. I've yet to fulfill my promise. A silent scream tears from me, but no one seems to care or notice. The shadows swirl and tighten around me, dragging me down into them, until I'm certain they'll drown me.

I open my mouth as darkness fills my vision, reaching out just as I fall backward.

I gasp, jolting awake as I press a hand to my pounding heart.

It was just a nightmare. My father is still safe, though I cannot say how Cyprian or my stepmother are faring.

One glance around the darkening shadows lets me know that Death has returned home. I sit up, smoothing out my hair, just as I hear the click of his boots against the stone floor as he approaches. Striding into the room, he stops short as his eyes land on me.

He'd been in the middle of peeling off his leather gloves, and I can't help the way my gaze lingers on his hands, eager for a glimpse of what lies beneath. I clear my throat, lifting my eyes to meet his when it becomes clear that his gloves are staying on.

Unable to contain my excitement at seeing him, I rise from the couch. A smile tugs at my lips as his shadows swirl around him. I see the confusion in his eyes as he stares at me.

He didn't expect to find me here, waiting for him, that much is clear. I hate that I haven't gone out of my way sooner to greet him and thank him for all that he's done for me.

"Welcome home," I say, adding an extra note of cheerfulness to my voice.

He's quiet for a long moment before giving me a nod in return.

I kick myself, realizing that he's probably not used to being greeted so cheerfully, let alone at all. I've probably just made things even more uncomfortable for him by doing so.

Fighting to keep the smile on my face, I take a step toward him, wondering if my presence is more disruptive to him than I'd realized. After all, it's pretty clear that this place has sat silent and empty for a very long time.

Perhaps that's exactly how he likes it and is now eager for it to return.

Especially when he's found the first guest that he's welcomed into his home in so long to be so ungrateful.

"I'm sorry," I say, the words spilling from me in a rush. "I'm sorry for not finding you sooner to thank you for what you've done, and the dresses. I only just saw them earlier. I truly do appreciate them—"

"Do not thank me," Death says, shifting uncomfortably on his feet. "It was the least I could do."

Clearly, this man has not been thanked enough for what he's done. I frown, realizing the true depth of this thought.

Of course, how many people can honestly say they've thanked Death for what he does? His job is a thankless one.

A hated one.

My heart tugs at the thought of how lonesome and thankless his life must be. Extra guilt piles on me that he must have assumed I was the same way. How could he not after how long it took me to get around to thanking him?

Chewing my lip, I watch him as he glances restlessly about the room before his gaze finally lands on me again. Our eyes meet, and the space between us suddenly feels heavy with all the unspoken words between us.

Forcing his eyes away from mine, he suddenly turns his back to me as if to leave the room.

"Wait," I call out, and he stops short, his shoulders tensing before he slowly pivots toward me. "There's something I want to show you. It won't take but a moment. Please?"

He cocks his head slightly to the side, his shadows swirling up with curiosity before finally giving me a small nod.

My smile brightens as I hurry over to him. Without thinking, I take his hand in mine as I lead him away from the sitting room. Death stiffens at my touch, but doesn't pull away, allowing me to drag him hand in hand through his own halls.

He falls into step beside me as we make our way through the empty halls. I can feel his eyes on me as we walk, not a word spoken between us, as his hand tightens around mine.

I keep my eyes trained ahead, warmth pooling through my body as I realize he's actually returned my touch for once.

Our silence is comfortable, and full of promise.

With each step closer, I feel my own excitement bubbling over. I can hardly wait to see what his reaction will be.

When we finally reach the door to my little studio, I pause with one hand on the door. Glancing back up at him, I find him watching me curiously as I pull in an excited breath.

"Now, close your eyes," I tell him. I wait a moment, suddenly realizing how hard it is to tell from here whether or not he's done as I've asked. "Are they closed?"

He nods once.

Grinning excitedly, I turn and push open the door, leading him into the room by his hand. Stopping in the middle of the room, I'm deliberate in the way I arrange him. His body stiffens with each touch of my hand, chills racing up and down my spine as his shadows swirl at my feet, but he doesn't so much as say a word to stop me.

Finally satisfied with his placement, I reluctantly drop my hands to my sides and take a step back. I want to be able to see his reaction, even if it's impossible to read much behind his mask.

"Okay," I say, "you can open your eyes now."

Slowly, Death drops his chin to stare at the painting sitting on the easel before him. Silence fills the room as I nervously wait with bated breath to hear what he thinks.

After all, it is a painting of him.

19

DEATH

I do not know how long I spend staring at the painting. I could stand here forever marveling its beauty.

The girl has managed to capture my likeness, my very essence, in a way no one ever has before, and I doubt will ever again. I have seen countless depictions of myself throughout the ages, but none has ever come so close. In fact, they pale in comparison to this.

This painting is altogether terrifying in its perfection, as though she has somehow managed to pull back my mask to reveal who I truly am.

Or, at least, who I try to be.

I find myself unable to do anything but stand and stare, at a complete and utter loss for words. I know I should say something, but I cannot seem to find my voice.

Every stroke of her brush seems to carry with it a piece of her soul, its song mixing with the paint and leaving behind fragments of itself. Showing me a side of her that I can only ever wish to see.

The care and precision in which she has painted me threatens to break me where no one has broken me before.

As I continue to stare at the painting, I silently pray that it does.

I adore this.

I adore *her*.

My heart aches at the very thought, as if it were near to bursting. Slowly, I shift my gaze to the girl.

She stands to one side, watching me with those great blue eyes of hers. They search my face, as though they can see through my mask. Through my entire being, and judging by her painting, in a way she has.

It is an uncomfortable thought, but not an entirely unwelcome one.

She beams up at me, her smile full of goodness, warmth, and sunshine. Full of everything that I am not. Everything that I never believed I could be part of, let alone enjoy.

Yet, seeing these things in her makes me want to lean into them, to welcome them into my life, and never let them go.

My eyes shift back to the painting as the silence continues to stretch between us, growing weightier with untold feeling as I struggle to form the words to tell her what this means to me. To praise her and the skill of, not just her hands, but her heart and soul.

But no words that come to mind seem to do her or the painting justice.

I despise that with each heartbeat that passes, I can feel fear wrapping around her as her eyes begin to flicker between the painting and me. Out of the corner of my eye, I see her expression waver.

My eyes meet hers just as fear takes hold, rising to meet me within the depths of her eyes, and I realize I have once again unintentionally wounded her.

My heart thuds sickeningly in my chest.

I do not know what to say to her, or how to express what her painting has done to me. So, instead, I turn on my heel and storm out of the room without a word.

Silence and space the only companions I know to keep my heart in check. The only way I know to escape the impossibility of this girl, of these emotions this mortal has forced upon me.

Each step further from the painting, from the girl, has my heart quickening and my mind racing.

This is not supposed to happen.

Not to me, and certainly not with a mortal.

I have always known the Fates to be cruel, but this ... this is a whole new degree of torture.

And yet, part of me wonders if they even know she is here when even I did not see her coming, or perhaps they sent her.

No matter how hard I try to reason with myself, try to explain away the girl and these feelings.

I cannot.

It does not matter that she is a mortal, who I myself have only promised death, my heart will no longer listen to reason.

It can no longer refuse to beat in rhythm with hers.

20

HAZEL

I fight back tears as I stare at the empty space where Death stood just moments ago.

My heart sinks as I try to understand what I've done wrong. Was he offended by my attempt at capturing his likeness?

I turn back to look at my painting, suddenly doubting myself. I had thought it my best work, but perhaps I was wrong.

Or perhaps, I've wronged him by trying to paint him at all. I am a mere mortal after all, and he ... well, far from it. I'm almost ashamed to admit that this thought hadn't even crossed my mind until now.

Either way, I need to make things right between us.

My heart tight, and my stomach knotting, I hurry after him. I just barely catch a glimpse of his billowing cloak disappearing around a corner as I leave the studio.

Trailing after his swirling shadows as they seem to get further and further away, I take in a breath as I pick up my skirts, quickening my pace. My boots pound against the marble of the halls as I race to catch up with him.

I have to make this right and fix whatever fracture I've created between us before he leaves again.

He seems to be moving impossibly fast, all too eager to put as much space between us and the disaster I've caused. My lungs burn for air as I run after him.

I lose sight of him several times, peering down dark, empty hallways as I chase any sign of him. Always at the last second, I seem to catch a flicker of movement or a particularly dark shadow to lead me in the right direction.

Or, so I hope.

For all I know, I could literally be chasing shadows.

Finally, my chase comes to an end when I suddenly find myself standing before a hall I've never noticed before. It's so truly hidden in shadow that it could easily pass for part of the wall.

I press on, moving through the swirling shadows that suddenly swallow me, and what little light there was, whole.

Forced to stop running, I raise my hands. One hand against the wall and the other lifted in front of me, I continue on through the darkness.

This isn't so different from the forest, and at least here I don't have to worry about the earth dragging me down into it. My steps falter at this, and I quickly shove the thought aside.

Death promised me no harm would come to me within these walls, and so far, he has kept his word.

Holding onto this promise, I move forward. Unable to

see, I'm forced to rely on small cues. The swish of a cloak as it whips around a corner, or the click of a heeled boot, the only signs that I'm heading in the right direction ... until I turn a corner.

Stopping, I blink, hardly daring to believe what I'm seeing.

At the far end of the hall is a cracked door, a soft glow spilling out from within. I quietly make my way toward it, hesitating for just a second before peering into the room.

It suddenly hits me that this must be his private wing of the palace, and this room ... his bed chamber.

I shouldn't be here. Everything that I've ever been taught about virtue and reputation screams at me to leave, but I don't.

Quietly, I push the door open and take a step inside.

Death's back is to me as he braces himself against the balustrade of his balcony across the room. An ocean of swirling mist fills the space beyond him, mixing with the chaos of his own shadows as they whip around him.

Again, that not so small part of me insists that I leave at once. It's clear that he wants to be alone, that he wants nothing to do with me.

But, again, I don't listen.

I continue to watch him from my spot just inside the door as he lifts one hand to remove the skull mask from his face. I clasp my hands over my mouth to stifle a gasp as he sets the mask down on the balustrade, his back still to me.

His mask removed, he runs a hand through his hair, pushing back a heavy hood to allow inky black hair to fall in messy waves down to his collar.

My heart skips a beat as I continue to stare, only belated realizing I've taken two steps closer to him, drawn forward by my own curiosity and concern. I don't need to see his face to know that whatever I've done to offend him weighs heavily upon him.

Death's shoulders are drawn tight as he grips the balustrade. He drops his chin with a sigh so deep that it has my heart breaking into a million pieces, his dark hair falling forward in a silky curtain around it.

I feel nauseous at the thought that I could have caused him this much distress.

Can I do anything at all right in this life or must I be a burden to all those around me? Perhaps it's best for everyone that my life will soon be cut short.

Realizing I've drawn even closer to him without thinking, I force myself to stop.

"Death?" I say, making my voice as soft as possible in an effort not to startle him.

His body stiffens for a moment before he slowly straightens to turn toward me.

My heartbeat quickens with sudden expectation before he catches himself. Reaching for the mask, his gloved fingers curl around it for a moment before he lifts it back to his face.

"Wait," I say, the words leaving me before I can stop myself. "Please, let me see your face."

He freezes, his hand still holding the mask to his face, and for just a breath, I think he will grant my request ... but then his body hardens, and he dons the mask in one quick motion.

Disappointment settles in my stomach at this, but I do my best to hide it as he pulls the hood up over his head and turns to face me.

"You should not be here," he says, his voice cutting me to my core.

I swallow past my emotions as I force myself to remain where I am.

He isn't wrong. In fact, he has every right to not want me here. I've gone against every instinct, every facet of human decency, to enter his bedroom uninvited.

I *know* I shouldn't be here, but I cannot leave things the way they are between us.

"I'm sorry."

He blinks at me, the shadows at his feet stilling momentarily as if I've just stunned him with my apology.

"I am sorry, truly," I continue, using his silence to plead my case. "If I have offended you. If the painting offended you, I will change it. I will destroy it if need be. I only meant to show my gratitude—"

"No," Death says, a strange edge to his voice that I haven't heard before.

Closing my mouth, I wait for him to continue, but the stillness between us only grows heavier as he refuses to look me in the eye.

"Please," I start again, when the silence is too much to bear any longer. "Please, tell me what I have done wrong so that I can fix it. I will give comfort where I have caused harm or reassurance where I have insulted. If only you will tell me."

He lets out a bitter laugh. Turning his back to me for a second, he lets out such a terrifying roar into the swirling mists beyond that it has me flinching as I stumble back a step.

Spinning back to face me, his eyes are wild, his chest heaving, as silence once again stretches between us. His shadows rise and fall, twisting around him as his eyes search my face, and I can only begin to imagine what he's about to say. The words he will use to tear into me and the painting he so clearly hates.

"You," he starts, taking one step closer. "You have undone me."

I blink up at him, unable to comprehend what his words mean. Is it possible that I misunderstood why he stormed off?

"I don't—"

"You captured my likeness in a way no one ever has before," he continues, the passion in his voice rooting me to the spot as he steps slowly toward me. "Through all my ages, I have never seen a more beautiful piece of art. And yet, beauty is too ugly a word to describe what I saw ... What I *see*. You gave me a glimpse into your soul, and the purity that I saw within burned me to my very core."

I must be misunderstanding him. I find it hard to believe that my painting could carry so much weight to it. Certainly, there must have been far greater artists, immortal even, who have captured his likeness better than I ever could.

"I'm afraid I don't understand."

"You deserve so much more than death," he says, closing the remaining distance between us as he reaches out to gently tilt my face toward him. "And yet, as things are, death is all that I am able to give you, Hazel."

21

HAZEL

The sound of my name on his lips leaves me breathless as I stare up at him, at a loss for words.

Taking a step back, my heart pangs with worry as I stare up at him. Is this his way of telling me that he means to go back on our deal?

My mouth runs dry as my breaths come quicker.

"Why are you telling me this?" I ask. "Do you not intend to follow through with our deal?"

"No, not at all," Death says, shaking his head slowly as he tries to close the distance between us. "My deals, once made, are final. The terms must be met. I only wished to convey how deeply I ... regret having to do it. I pray the one you are saving is truly worth the price you are going to pay."

"He is," I answer without hesitation. "My father is a good man, kind, and well worth my sacrifice. He has spent much of his life helping others, and I know he will continue to do so. Saving him is the best use I could make of my soul and life. Without him, I would have no life, no future to live."

Death's eyes narrow on me, seemingly unconvinced. I search my mind, struggling to come up with a way to prove it to him.

"I do not think you know the value of your own soul," he says.

I blink up at him, his words forming a lump at the back of my throat. Shaking my head, I drop my eyes to the floor as tears blur my vision.

"You are mistaken," I whisper. "My soul is worth nothing save for this one act. Ask anyone who knows me, and they'll agree. Father is a light in a sea of darkness, and a man many would mourn the loss of. Unlike me."

Death is quiet for a long moment before reaching out to brush the tears from my cheeks, his touch making my heart skip another beat.

"I would mourn your loss, little one," he says quietly. "So, forgive me, but I must see for myself if your claims are true."

It takes a second for his words to sink in. As soon as they do, hope and excitement spark to life within me.

"Yes," I say, my worry lessening, "you will understand as soon as you see him. I'm sure of it."

There's a little part of me that worries he won't see what I see now that Father lies sick in bed, but perhaps he can see more than even he lets on. I'm curious how he intends to peer into the life I left behind, and whether or not I'll be able to catch a glimpse of it, too.

206

There must be some way these immortals check in on our lives, right?

As he moves past me, I let my imagination run wild. Perhaps there's a mist-covered pool or a magic mirror that allows him to see whatever it is he pleases in the other realms. If I'm lucky, he might even let me use it too. Then, I could check in on Father, and even Cyprian, to make sure they were okay.

It's only when Death reaches into his wardrobe and pulls out a new cloak that I realize there's no such magic pool. He intends to go to my village, my home, and see my family with his own eyes.

A little of my excitement dies at this. I had hoped for a chance to see Father myself, and to make sure that he was still breathing and that all was well at home, or as well as it could be in my absence.

Part of me still worries that I bargained my soul too late. That by the time the new moon comes, and Death becomes aware of my mistake, my father will have long since been buried.

What would happen to me then?

My mind begins to spiral, and I have to force myself to refocus as I follow Death through palace halls. I chew my lip, far too many questions forming in my mind as we walk.

I'm curious how he leaves this place, and what he sees when he does.

Is it all darkness and swirling mist for him out there, too? Does he always end up in that strange forest? What will he see when he visits my home? Will he share any news with me, or must he keep everything he sees to himself?

Honestly, regarding this last thought, I'm not sure that I want him to. I doubt Merelda has taken great care of the house, let alone the garden or animals, and I can only *hope* that she's been tending to Father as she should.

And I hate to think what's come of Cyprian.

Reaching the main entryway, my steps slow as Death strides toward the large front doors. I watch him, half expecting him to leave without so much as a farewell, but then he turns to look at me.

His gaze cuts through me, a little blossom of hope rising in my chest as he motions me closer.

"Tell me, little one, where exactly might I find your home?"

"You do not know?"

"Despite what most mortals think, I am not an all-knowing creature," he answers. "Each day that I step into your world, it is simply to heed the call of the dying. Unless I know exactly what I want and where I want it from, my only reason for stepping into your world is to seek out the souls of the marked, the dying, and the damned."

I'm surprised by this, and can't help but think it sounds a little sad and lonely. He may be free to go anywhere in the world, but what use is it when only the dead and the damned await you on the other side?

I think if I were him, I would be all too eager to fill my home with color and warmth, especially if my days were otherwise filled with death and mourning.

"My home is located just a few miles northwest of the

small town of Caravath," I answer. "It sits atop a small hill, surrounded by a forest and a neighboring apple orchard."

I frown, wondering what else might help him distinguish whether or not he is at the right house.

"What is your father's name?" Death asks, as if reading my thoughts.

"Leoric Goodwin."

"Hmm." He pauses for a moment, as if mulling over the information I've given him before nodding once. "Thank you, that will do."

"Then you already know how to get there?"

"Yes."

I chew my as he turns to leave before blurting out, "If you find a small book along the way, would you mind bringing it back to me? I think I may have lost it in the woods the night we met."

He stops, halfway to the doors, his back still to me as he considers my request.

"Of course."

"I wish I could accompany you," I quickly add.

He pauses, his hand now on the door, before answering, "As do I, little one."

The next second, he's thrown open one of the doors and stepped out into the swirling mist, letting it slam closed with a heavy thud behind him. I stare after him for a long moment, half hoping he'll return and take me with him.

But even I know that's impossible.

I feel the loss of his presence as I move to press a hand to the doors, and can't help but hope his journey is swift. Despite knowing that he's traversed the realms numerous times, never mind the simple fact that he isn't mortal, I find myself anxiously awaiting his safe return.

With a sigh, I step back from the door. Turning on my heel, I walk through the empty halls. The lone click of my boots does little to lift my spirits as I return to my studio.

Stepping inside, I set Death's painting aside, replacing it with a blank canvas. I stare at the empty space for a long time, but find myself without my usual desire to create.

My mind seems unwilling to release me from its swirling thoughts. Settling onto my stool, I wrap my cloak around me in a warm hug as tears wet my cheeks.

I know I promised myself I wouldn't wallow in despair, but I need a moment to grieve. A moment to process the fact that I will never see my father again.

In a way, it's a relief to let myself crumble into a million pieces. Grief is quick to sweep in, but I don't let it drown me. Instead, I give myself permission to feel, to let go of my anguish. It's too great of a burden to continue hiding it within my chest.

I need to let go, or I fear that by the end of my time here, I will be nothing more than a husk of myself.

What's done is done, and I truly do not regret the choice I've made.

If I hadn't come here, Father would have died, and I would have been sold off to Lord Payne to be miserable until the last of my days. This way, all of that has been avoided, and Father will have many happy years ahead of him.

Still, Death is right about the value of life, and I will not allow myself to waste what little of it I have left. As long as I still draw breath, I intend to make the most of my time here, whether it be alone or by Death's side.

Drying my tears, I straighten and reach for a brush, dipping it into a small pot of paint. Without further hesitation, I set to work with newfound vigor.

As my brush sweeps across the canvas, all else soon fades into the background of my mind.

Once again, days seem to slip past as I await Death's return, my paintbrush my only constant companion.

I work late into the evening, only breaking for food during the day. Each night, I return to my bedroom to bathe and curl up beneath the thick furs to sleep.

Morning brings with it a new choice of dress, as well as the anticipation of Death's imminent return. Hope and expectation sparking new and grander ideas each time I return to my art.

I paint until there is no more room to work, every inch of space in my studio filled with my art in various stages of drying. When I finally take a step back to admire everything I've created, I feel an overwhelming sense of satisfaction.

In just the short time I've been here, I've managed to create in a way I never have before. Bringing to life more ideas and visions than I even thought possible.

Many of the paintings depict places that I once traveled to with Father, others are simply stolen from daydreams. Each piece is filled with warmth, joy, and the vibrancy of life ...

Exactly what this palace is missing.

Realizing that my paintings should no longer be

constrained to this one room, I set out to hang them throughout the empty rooms and halls.

My time here may be limited, but I intend to leave a piece of myself behind for Death. So that, hopefully, he will never have to feel so cold or alone here again.

As I hang each of my pieces, I feel a little bit of warmth and life spread throughout the palace. I'm unable to stop the smile that pulls at my lips as I work.

Until I'm only left with one final piece.

Death's portrait.

I stare at it for a long moment, wondering where I should hang it. It seems appropriate to hang it in the main room, centered over the fireplace, but I cannot bring myself to do it. Perhaps a more intimate setting, such as his private chambers, would be more suitable ...

I blush at the thought of my painting hanging over his bed before dismissing it almost immediately.

Sighing, I realize that I'm simply reluctant to have it gone from my studio.

Centering it on my easel, I tilt my head to one side as I run my eyes over Death's form before reaching for my paintbrush once again.

No, I'm quite ready to part with this one.

Not yet.

22

DEATH

I stand outside the quaint little house, my eyes slowly taking it all in. On the surface, it is surprisingly charming for a human home, though a bit overgrown for my taste. However, a darkness has settled over it that has my lip curling up in disgust.

My shadows twist around me in displeasure.

This is not a house of welcoming, not a darkness born of pain and necessity, but one of brutality and hate.

Where I must be cruel for the sake of those around me, there is joy taken from it here.

No, this darkness holds no beauty.

As I move closer, the true state of the girl's home becomes ever more apparent, and I wonder how she could have ever lived in a place like this.

Sighing deeply, I step into the house.

A woman paces next to a cold fireplace, her hands tearing at her hair as she talks to herself. I watch her quietly, the darkness that rolls off her in heavy waves, sickening.

"That stupid girl," the woman mutters to herself. "As soon as I find her, I will make her rue the very day she was born. Lord Payne will be the least of her worries, mark my words."

I take a step closer, allowing my presence to fill the room as if daring her to continue.

She pauses, her brow furrowing, as she slowly turns toward me. I see fear flicker in her eyes, though I know she cannot see me.

Not unless I wish it.

Still, I enjoy saturating the room with myself, letting her feel the cold touch of death wafting about her. My shadows leech toward her, wrapping around her ankles and slithering their way up her body.

I want her to know what *true* power feels like. How inconsequential she is when faced with it.

She shudders, and the corner of my mouth twitches. Frowning, I pull back, and she lets out a small sigh of relief as she leans against the mantle. A second later, she straightens, the cruelty returning to her face.

"When I get my hands on that girl," she spits, "I'll strangle her to within an inch of her life. No, I will draw her death out slowly. Lord Payne will simply be the first of her tormentors. I'll let him use her until she's nearly broken, and then I'll drag the brat out from under him and away to another. Never again will she know love or kindness. She will only know pain and hate, until her body and soul finally break. Hazel will pay for what she's done to my family, and I will be there to watch every moment of it."

My hands curl into fists at my side, the leather of my gloves tightening as I force myself to remain where I am. To not reach out and rip the soul from her body.

Taking a deep breath, I glare down at the woman before turning my back to her.

No, death would be a kindness when it comes to giving this woman what she truly deserves.

A gift I am not yet willing to give her.

Moving through the house, I can see traces of Hazel's presence. However, it is obvious from the layer of dust and grime that her absence has been missed, and it repulses me to think how her time was used here.

Making my way up to the second floor, I stare down a long hallway. Closing my eyes, I let myself feel the house, the rooms, the call of other souls. My shadows flow along the walls, dipping beneath the doors as they fill the house.

Then my heart thuds twice.

Two souls, one of which is far weaker than the other. However, there is something about the first that has my chest tightening.

Something familiar.

Opening my eyes, I momentarily push away the feeling as I move deeper into the house. Stopping in front of one of the doors, I open it and step into a stiflingly hot bedroom.

My skin crawls, the heat clawing at me as I force myself further into the room. With a wave of my hand, my shadows burst through the room, devouring the heat, and leaving an icy chill in their wake.

Satisfied with the change in atmosphere, I turn toward the bed to see a man lying still and pale beneath far too many quilts. Approaching the bed, I find him to be in a state as close to death as the bargain will allow.

She came to me not a moment too soon. Had she stepped back out, had she chosen not to stay with me, this man would already be dead.

Frowning, I crouch beside the bed.

Her father does not so much as flutter an eyelid, his chest barely able to rise and fall. I will myself to see past his outward appearance and into his soul. Will myself to see what Hazel sees in this dying mortal.

This man whom she has chosen to give up her life for.

Closing my eyes, I reach out a gloved hand to touch him. A tingle of pain shoots through my arm, but subsides to a dull throb a moment later. My mind, my shadows, search him, call to him.

The soul that answers is warm, but pales in comparison to hers. Where his light is a soft, fading glow, hers burns brighter than the many suns.

But within him, I also see the kindness she mentioned. The care he has poured into others. The love he feels for *her*.

Our Hazel.

Sighing, I pull my hand back as I rise to my feet. Staring down at him, I realize she will never understand the depth of what she has done. What she has given up for this man.

She will never see what I see, what I feel, in her.

This man will live, only because of what she has sacrificed, but for how long?

My shadows shift, drawing my attention to the night-stand. Glancing down, my eyes narrow on a half-full cup on top of it.

Lifting it to my face, my nose wrinkles at the subtle mixture of scents within. Sifting through them, it takes me a moment to recognize what is wrong with it.

Poisoned, and no doubt administered by the wretched creature downstairs.

Hazel never said a word about how terrible the rest of her family is. How much suffering she endured in this home.

It is a testament to the purity of her soul, yet it fills me with rage.

The situation is impossible.

This man will survive what his wife has done to him, only because of his daughter's actions.

But her sacrifice will be in vain. As long as he allows that woman whom he calls wife to remain, he will certainly die before too long.

Pivoting on my heel, I sweep from the room. My glove half removed as I stride toward the stairs, fully intent on draining the very life from the woman myself. The Fates will never let me hear the end of it for taking her life before her time, but to hell with them.

I only stop short when my shadows suddenly dip beneath another door, reminding me of the other soul in Hazel's home.

My jaw hardening, I struggle to ignore it, but find I cannot. Pulling my glove back on, I enter a second bedroom to find a young man sitting on the floor against the bed.

He reeks of alcohol and sorrow, his clothes and body caked in dried blood and dirt. I frown, wondering why I felt drawn to him at all. Human sorrow means little to me. This world is fleeting, their lives mere moments in the great expanse of time.

I start to turn when my eyes catch on something in the man's hand, and my heart stills in my chest.

Shadows burst from me to fill the room once again. Gesturing toward the man, I watch as my shadows momentarily steal the breath from his lungs, the small paper slipping from his hand as his body freezes in time.

Stepping forward, I bend to pick it up, my eyes tracing the small illustration.

It is a drawing of her, torn from a book, a single inscription written upon it.

To my darling, Hazel. I wish you the happiest of birthdays, with all the love this world has to offer.

Rage blinds me as I stare down at it, my vision darkening.

Love?

Who is this man to her? What gives him the right to feel this way about her?

She never mentioned a lover.

My fist crumples around the paper as I move to shove it into my pocket, only to remember the book tucked within.

No.

Hesitating, I pull the book out, turning it over in my hand before slowly opening the cover to find a missing page. My stomach twisting, I smooth out the crumpled illustration to align the jagged edges.

A perfect fit.

My heart quiets as ice begins to creep back in around it.

Of course, what a fool I have been. To think that her kindness toward me could ever be more than that. I have mistaken her friendship for more, and by no fault of her own.

Her heart belongs to another, and I am but a means to an end.

That is all.

Tossing the drawing to the floor, I tuck the book back inside my pocket before fleeing the room, my shadows in tow.

My mind warns me against it, and yet, I cannot stop myself from seeking out Hazel's room. Though she can never be mine, at least I can fill my memory with her.

At the back of the house, I find a small bedroom. There are few possessions within, and my heart breaks as I take it all in.

From the worn mattress to the threadbare blanket, it is clear that she was mistreated while she lived here. The room itself is barren and uncomfortable, with a leak in the far corner, yet, her lingering presence still saturates the room with warmth.

I frown as my thoughts darken.

How could her father allow her to be treated in such a manner? And what of this so-called lover?

Why did he not protect her?

The room alone is evidence enough of her mistreat-ment. Though there are small details of her left behind, a pressed daisy in the window and a comb next to the bed, it is clear that her existence was barely tolerated here.

I cannot help but wonder what type of man would allow his daughter to be treated in such a way. Regardless of his soul, if he is truly the kind and caring man that Hazel has made him out to be, then he has yet to prove it to me.

Turning my back on her old room, I storm from the house and make my way back toward the small town and tavern

I need time to think. To understand who these people are and process what I have learned before I can return home to Hazel.

Time to quiet my feelings, before I do something utterly unforgivable.

23

HAZEL

I'm balancing on a chair, struggling to hang a landscape I've just finished painting above the main sitting room fireplace, when an icy chill rushes over me. Pausing in my work, I turn to glance over my shoulder.

Haunting the doorway is the looming silhouette of Death.

"You're back!" I say giving him a bright smile.

He says nothing as his eyes shift from me to slowly take in the painting I'm holding. My cheeks flush as he steps closer.

"I hope you don't mind. I was running out of space to put them in the studio. I know I should have asked before I started hanging them, but—"

"I love it," he says, cutting me off as he moves to stand beside me. Taking the painting from me, he lifts it into place above the mantle. My heart races at his closeness, and I have to stop myself from reaching for him. From telling him how much I've missed him.

He steps back, his eyes shifting back to me.

"Did you find my father?" I ask quietly.

"I did."

"And how is he?" I press when he doesn't elaborate further.

He hesitates for a moment, his gaze returning to the painting before flickering back to me.

"He is alive."

I watch him as his attention once again shifts to the painting.

He's obviously holding something back. How else could he be gone for so long only to return with such a vague response?

Worrying my lip, I wait for him to tell me more.

I don't want to press him, but I'm curious about the life I left behind. Has Father begun to improve? Is Cyprian okay? Have I been blamed for Amadeus' death?

Finally, when I realize that he intends to give me no further details, I force a bright smile onto my face.

"Are you hungry?"

He snorts softly in surprise at my question.

"You know I do not hunger in the way you mortals do," he says, pausing as he takes in my expression. "But, I suppose, I could eat."

"Perfect," I say, brightening again, "The stew should be just about finished."

He offers his hand to me as I move to get off the chair, and I accept, the frost of his touch mixing with the burning heat in my chest as he helps me down. He drops my hand the moment I'm safely on the floor, and I try my best not to show my disappointment.

Death follows me through the halls, his eyes trailing over the various paintings that now adorn his walls. Our pace is slow as he takes his time admiring each piece, his eyes sparkling through his mask as he stares at my work. Despite him not saying a word, my cheeks are sore from fighting back an ever-widening smile by the time we reach the kitchen.

The warm scent of cooked vegetables and herbs wafts up around us, and I instinctively turn to look up at Death. He gives me a gracious nod, his only acknowledgment that the aroma is as pleasing to him as it is me.

Warmth pools within me, my heart full, as I step toward the fire to check on the bubbling stew. Behind me, Death moves to settle on the same stool the first, and only other time that we shared a meal in here.

I ladle out two bowls of stew before reaching for the small loaf of bread I baked earlier in the hopes that he would return.

"Here," I say, setting the bread and bowl of stew down next to him before returning for my own.

Settling onto the stool beside him, I watch as he dips his spoon into the steaming bowl. I can't help myself, secretly hoping he'll finally remove his mask to eat.

But he doesn't.

He drops his head forward to allow him to slip the spoon beneath the mask without me seeing.

I have to reign in my disappointment yet again, as I turn my focus toward my own bowl.

A comfortable silence stretches between us as we eat. The stew is perfect and warms me from the cold wafting off Death. He seems content as he finishes his first bowl before standing and retrieving a second.

I can't help the feeling of joy that fills me as I watch him help himself. I know that for a creature that doesn't need food the same way that I do, him having a second bowl is high praise indeed.

As he finishes his second bowl, and I my first, I can feel the space between us growing heavier as he stares into his empty bowl.

"Why did you never mention the cruelty that you endured at the hands of your family?" he suddenly asks, shattering the silence between us.

His question startles me. It was certainly not one I thought he'd ever ask, let alone *know* to ask. Was it really that obvious from a simple visit to my home?

"I ... Well, I didn't think it was necessary," I start. "They made my life harder, but it was nothing I couldn't endure, for the sake of my Father's happiness. He deserved to be happy. I wanted him to be happy, whatever the cost to my own."

The shadows darken around Death, and I know he's not content with my answer. When I finally brave a glance up at him, his black eyes are burning with a fire I've never seen in them before.

Swallowing down the fear that claws its way into my chest, I refuse to look away.

"His *happiness* came at the expense of your own, and

you were all right with that?" he asks, his voice thick with displeasure.

"You do not know the life we lived before … it seemed a small price to pay for me to see him happy again."

"You alone should have been all the happiness he needed, Hazel."

Again, the sound of my name on his lips has my heart skipping a beat and leaves me wishing to hear him say it over and over again. And yet, his other words pain me.

I hate how desperately I wish they were true, but that isn't how the world works. I was but his daughter; I could never bring him the intimacy our fragile hearts crave.

As much as he loved me, I knew that I was still a burden to him. Though he would never admit it.

When he brought Merelda into our lives, I know it was done out of love for me as much as it was companionship for himself. As foolish as his choice turned out to be.

"I do not see how that matters," I finally say.

"How can you not?" he says, his voice growing sharper. "You sacrificed yourself for his happiness. You have spent your whole life in suffering, and no one cared to save you, let alone protect you."

"It was my life to do with as I saw fit," I answer. "I do not regret the choices I have made."

"He is not worthy of your sacrifice. Your life was wasted—"

"Who are *you* to judge me?" I retort, a fire suddenly flaring to life within me. "What is it that you do with your own life? What sacrifices have you made for the ones you love? If you've ever known love at all."

I regret this last comment the moment it leaves my mouth, but I'm too consumed with anger to immediately take them back.

Death lets out a low growl that rumbles through me, allowing me to actually feel the depth of his anger.

Well, good. Now we can both be upset.

I don't appreciate the way he stares at me, as if he's personally offended by my choices. It wasn't like I had much choice in the life I was given, and still, I tried my best. Tried to be a good daughter, tried to bear Merelda's cruelty if only it meant Father was happy. Tried to keep my mother's dying wishes.

Gods, all I did was try to make everyone else happy.

Why should I be berated for that?

"You deserved better," Death says coldly. "You *deserve* better."

I have to bite back a laugh at this.

"Perhaps, but it was not what fate had in store for me. I did what I thought best, and I do not see how you can sit there and judge me for it."

"I am not judging you."

"Then what would you call it?"

"I simply do not wish for you to throw away your life for this man."

"He is my father, and it is my life to do with as I please. Our deal still stands, does it not?"

"It does, but—"

"Then my decision is final. I see no point in getting caught up in the details of my past. I am here now, and I will not have you try to change my mind."

A strange mixture of emotions crashes through me, bringing tears of frustration to my eyes. I hate how easily he saw into the pain of my past, how easily he tore down the walls I'd spent my whole life building.

I hate that he recognized how bitter life had been for me, and how he doesn't agree with the choice I've made.

But, worst of all, I hate how much I desperately *want* him to convince me to change my mind.

"Hazel," Death says, his voice soft.

I shake my head, leaping to my feet to storm out of the kitchen before he can say another word. Afraid that if he does, if I hear my name fall from his lips once more, that I will break for him.

Despite the recent years of misery, Father and I shared many happy years together, and I will do anything to make sure he has many more ahead. I cannot allow Death to change that.

Running through the palace halls, I find myself standing before my studio. Entering, I let the door slam heavily behind me before I let out a small sob.

Who does he think he is to sit there and judge my life? What does he have to offer me but death and heartbreak?

I turn to face the door as I consider locking it, but I decide against it. I doubt if he truly wanted to, it would keep him out anyway ... and then, there's still that small part of me that hopes he'll come for me.

That he'll convince me to change my mind. That he'll offer me a life that I simply cannot refuse.

It sounds foolish, and I feel disgust at myself even

thinking it. Sighing, I wipe the tears from my eyes as I move toward my easel, placing a new canvas on it.

There's a soft knock on the door as I reach for a paintbrush.

I go still, my heart pounding in my chest as I wait for him to burst into the room. But he simply calls out to me.

I frown, trying my best to ignore him. It should matter very little to me what he has to say. Anything he says is just to convince me that I'm being a fool.

No, it would be far more foolish of me to think that a man such as himself, a monster, could care about me.

Could want me.

"Hazel," he calls again. "I did not mean to upset you. Please, I simply ... I simply wish that you would reconsider."

"It's a little too late for that, is it not?" I answer, knowing he will hear the bitterness in words despite the door between us. "My fate is sealed if I wish my father to live, is it not?"

His silence is all the confirmation I should need to know that I'm right. I should be furious that he's trying to change my mind. I should know better than to think he actually cares.

For all I know, he's simply trying to find a way to collect both my father's soul and mine. For all I know, he's pretending to care.

He is *death*.

Still, I find myself waiting with bated breath for him to answer. I hate that I want him to tell me that, no, my fate is not sealed.

"Yes," he finally responds.

Biting back tears of disappointment that startle me, I swallow hard.

"Then go, and leave me to finish out my days in peace."

"As you wish."

A long moment passes before I hear his heavy footsteps retreating from my door. I hold myself still until I can no longer hear him.

Then I break.

Crumbling to the floor, my hands come to my face as heavy sobs rack my body. I curl around myself, drawing my cloak tighter as I let the tears come until exhaustion takes me

Sleep the only thing that finally soothes the agony of my heart.

24

HAZEL

Clarity returns in the morning as I open my eyes to stare up at my blank canvas.

Sitting up, I know what I must do. I cannot leave things between Death and I as they currently stand.

I had not meant to sleep on the floor of my studio, but I did not have the energy or desire to drag myself to bed last night. Dragging my aching body off the floor, I move toward the door. Exhaustion pulls at me, and I find myself having to lean against the wall to catch my breath.

I must have slept even more poorly than I thought.

Brushing the back of my hand across my forehead, I realize I'm sticky with sweat, my hair clinging to my face and neck.

I'm desperate to seek Death out, but not like this. I must bathe and change, and then go to him as quickly as I can before he finds a reason to leave.

Somehow, deep down, I know that he's still here,

walking the halls of his palace. I don't know what to make of this feeling, but I decide some things are best left alone, and instead simply allow myself to be grateful for this strange knowing.

Opening the door to my studio, I stop short as I discover a parcel laying on the floor. Bending to pick it up, I find a note attached to a single marigold ... just like the ones that grow in the garden at home.

I allow myself a moment to appreciate its beauty before opening the note.

If you are willing, put this on and meet me downstairs at your earliest convenience.

-D

I trace the single scrawling letter of his name, suddenly reminded of my wish to give him another, before turning my attention to the parcel in my arms. Carefully pulling loose the ribbon, it falls open to reveal an even more beautiful dress than all the ones I've been given so far.

It's made from a silk so black it resembles wet ink, and I find myself thrilled at the prospect of wearing it.

Before I even realize it, I'm halfway back to my room. With his gift held tight to my chest, I move through the halls as fast as I can.

I bathe as thoroughly and quickly as I can before carefully stepping into the new dress.

I was wrong. This dress isn't made of silk, but a material I'm completely unfamiliar with. The fabric hugs my body, falling elegantly to my ankles as it moves not altogether dissimilarly to the shadows that cling to Death.

I glance at myself in the mirrored wall, stunned by how lovely the dress is. It almost feels as if I'm wearing nothing, fitting so well that I have to run my hands over it to remind myself that I am, in fact, wearing anything at all.

Of course, this means that I'm shivering within minutes. The dress, as lovely as it is, offers little warmth, and I have to reach for my cloak before I freeze to ... Well, before I freeze.

Sinking into the warmth of the cloak, I smile as I reach for the flower on my bed and tuck it into my cloak before leaving my room to make my way downstairs.

Death paces anxiously at the bottom of the sweeping staircase, only stopping when he looks up to see me.

"Hazel," he says softly, his eyes meeting mine and nearly stealing my breath away.

He's dressed in a form-fitting outfit today, the black fabric similar to my own as it accentuates the ungodly perfection of his build. Even his mask seems to fit more snugly, his hair allowed to fall in loose waves around it, as he watches me descend the stairs.

He truly is beautiful, even with his face entirely hidden from me.

Reaching the bottom steps, he holds out a gloved hand toward me.

I hesitate for a moment, staring up at him before taking his hand as I close the remaining distance between us.

His hand swallows mine as he wastes no time pulling

me closer, tucking me into his side as his other hand moves to wrap around my waist.

"Thank you," I say, his touch nearly making me forget my manners, "for the dress and the flower. I adore them both."

Death makes a small sound of acceptance, but stiffens slightly at my gratitude.

"I would like to share something with you," he says softly, the shadows dancing excitedly around him as he leads me through the halls of the palace.

It feels so intimate to be this close to him, pressed against the cold muscle of his body. Never have I been this close to another and felt so pleasantly content.

As we walk, I bite my cheek to keep myself from asking him where he's taking me. If he wanted me to know, he would have told me, and I refuse to allow myself to spoil the surprise for either of us.

Still, I can't help stealing glances up at his masked face as we walk. Finally, we come to stand before a set of deep black doors that I've never seen before. I frown slightly as he shifts away from me to push open the heavy doors with both hands.

I peer past him into the world beyond where a set of stairs seems to disappear as it leads down into the ocean of mist that I've come to know all too well.

"You will not need your cloak where we are going, little one," he says. "You may take it off and leave it here."

"Okay," I say after a moment's hesitation, a chill already working its way through me at the thought.

I start to raise my hand to do as he's asked, but he stops

me as he steps closer to undo the clasp for me instead. My eyes don't leave his face as he lets the cloak slip from my shoulders to pool at my feet.

A sharp intake of air, his only reaction to seeing me in the dress he gave me. His eyes shift lower as they take me in, the way he looks at me with such appreciation, causing warmth to flood my cheeks.

Until his eyes suddenly harden.

"What's wrong?" I ask, taking a step back just as he reaches out to stop me.

His other hand lifts to brush back the hair that's fallen over my shoulder to reveal the scar from Payne's ring.

"Who did this to you?"

"It's nothing—"

"I asked, who did this to you?"

"Lord Payne," I answer. "It was his way of marking me as his betrothed."

Death's grip tightens slightly around my arm as his shadows swell around him.

"Your betrothed," he says, sounding slightly confused by this. "Tell me, little one, does this *Lord Payne* reside in your town?"

"Yes, well, just a few miles south of it, but please don't allow what he did to spoil our day. He means nothing to me. He never meant anything to me."

It takes a moment for his grip on my arm to ease. Stepping back, he clears his throat once before offering his hand to me again.

"Very well, let us put this matter aside for the time being."

"Thank you," I say, slipping my hand into his.

"Now, hold on tight."

Turning, he leads me out of his palace, and I cling to him, taking unabashed pleasure in being able to do so. Together, we step forward as one.

The mist immediately wraps around us, obscuring everything else and leaving me wondering if the world has simply fallen away. If not for the solid form of Death at my side, I'd be terrified that the mist might sweep me away as it crashes around us.

Another step, and I'm unable to see anything other than the wild swirling of the mist as it dances around us. It would be so easy to be lost forever amidst this ocean of mist. My grip tightens on Death's hand at this thought, and he pulls me closer to him as we continue our descent.

I quickly lose track of time, unable to see anything, even Death at my side. By the time we finally step out of the mist, it feels like an eternity has passed, though I'm sure it couldn't have been more than a few moments.

I have to squint, blinded by the brightness of the light here after becoming so accustomed to darkness. One glance over my shoulder confirms that the mist still looms there, waiting for us to take a step back so it can reclaim us. A shiver works its way through me at the thought of having to traverse it again before I turn away.

My eyes still adjusting, my breath catches in my throat as I take the scene before me. I can feel my eyes widen, and the way my lips part in awe as I stare out at the golden plain that stretches as far as I can see. Bright white flowers in full bloom are speckled about, dancing lazily with a soft breeze.

"Where are we?" I ask, my eyes catching on distant trees far off on the horizon and colors that I don't even have a name for.

Death says nothing as we stand, hand in hand looking out over the land.

A soft, warm breeze sweeps through, causing the golden grass before us to sway, and I let out a contented sigh as it washes over my skin. Closing my eyes, I tilt my head back for a moment, inhaling the sweet, floral-scented air.

Releasing my hand, Death takes a step forward. He is still close enough that I can feel the chill of his shadow lingering on me, but it's offset by whatever this magical place is.

Opening my eyes, I look up to find Death watching me, the inky darkness of his eyes somehow even more unsettling here. Something makes me want to reach for him, to gently lift his mask to give light to whatever darkness lies beneath.

But I don't.

Tearing his eyes from me, he turns his back to me and lets out a whistle so loud and sharp that it causes me to flinch. The sound echoes into the distance before it's suddenly replaced by the thunder of approaching hooves.

Peering out into the field, my heart skips a beat in my chest as I watch the most magnificent stallion I've ever seen race toward us. His white coat shines in the sun, his mane billowing out behind him as the light seems to cast a golden halo around him.

The stallion comes to a thundering stop before us, tossing his mane and rearing up into the sky, and Death takes my hand, startling my attention back to him as his touch sends an icy jolt through my body.

Glancing between him and the massive stallion, I can almost imagine him smiling behind his mask.

"Welcome, Hazel," he says, pulling me closer, "to the Valley of Death, and my horse."

25

DEATH

Hazel brightens, her soul singing to me as she smiles up at me before turning back to the valley.

There is so much I would like to tell her about this place. So much I would like to show her, but I hesitate. I have never shared this place with anyone before, mortal or otherwise, and seeing her here now ... terrifies me.

Her presence amplifies the power and beauty of this place in a way I have never felt before, and yet, she is oblivious to it.

Her joy flows into me, searing me with the heat of her body, but I do not pull away. I would rather endure a thousand ages of pain than let her go.

My heart aches as I realize this is exactly what I will have to do in far too short a time.

Hazel smiles as she watches my stallion toss his head as he nickers in greeting toward me, still I do not pull my eyes from her. The warmth of her smile reminding me of summer days I thought long lost to me.

Not knowing what to make of my emotions, I say nothing, allowing us both a moment to simply be.

"What is his name?" Hazel asks, her eyes briefly returning to mine.

Knax paws the ground, shaking his mane as if offended by her question. I snort, reaching out to pat a hand against his withers to soothe his bruised ego.

"His name is Knax," I answer, as he tosses his head back again. "Though, I suppose there are many interpretations of his name through the ages."

"Knax," she repeats, his name coming out in a whisper as she stares up at him before taking a tentative step forward.

I watch, allowing her to pull away from me as she reaches a small, trembling hand out toward my horse. He stills as she draws closer, allowing her a single pat before shuffling away from us with a loud snort.

I feel her momentary disappointment crash over me before a surprised giggle bubbles out of her. And, again, her happiness tugs at the strings of my heart.

"He is not the friendliest of creatures," I warn as she takes another step away from me toward Knax.

She glances back at me, determination shining bright in her eyes.

"He just doesn't know me yet," she says before turning back to slowly work her way toward him.

"I have known him for many millennia," I call out, "and he still barely tolerates me."

She ignores my comment, reaching out once more as she draws near to him again. Once again, Knax stills long enough to allow her a single touch before whinnying and galloping a short distance away.

I cannot help the low chuckle that spills from me as I watch her attempt to pet him yet again, though I cut it short, surprised by the unusual feeling of the sound reverberating through my chest.

"We will be friends, Knax," Hazel insists before shooting a cheerful smile over her shoulder at me.

With the sunlight haloing her, Hazel's beauty steals my breath from me. It takes all my self-control to remain where I am, watching as her soul's song reaches a crescendo within me. Everything about her is amplified here, the true depths of her innocence and purity reaching ungodly heights.

If I could just freeze this moment in time, I would.

Watching as she approaches my horse again, I am shocked when she is allowed three pats this time. Though, perhaps I should not be surprised.

After all, she seems to have a knack for warming the hearts of even the coldest creatures to her.

Hazel's laughter fills the valley as she and Knax fall into a rhythm of give and take. She seems perfectly content with the small moments he gives her, each touch bringing a new smile to her lips.

It is hard to ignore how perfectly she fits in here. Even Knax seems to be warming to her, allowing her more pats each time she catches him.

"I think he likes you."

She spins around to beam at me, and my heart thuds painfully in my chest.

"Do you really think so?" she asks, running a hand over Knax's muzzle.

He gives me a snort to let me know he is simply tolerating her for my sake, but he makes no move to distance himself from her.

Just as I have not.

Stepping closer to stand by Hazel's side, I wrap an arm under and around Knax's head to pull him to my chest. I press my forehead to his for a moment before releasing him. He whinnies, and I reach for Hazel. Guiding her hand over Knax's flank as my eyes fall to her.

I cannot help but admire her patience with Knax, or the softness in her voice as she whispers to him of his beauty and strength.

She is an impossibility in this universe of suffering.

"Come," I say after another moment, stepping back.

She glances up at me, obviously reluctant to leave Knax's side, and he gives her a soft snort as if to promise her that he will remain nearby. This seems to satisfy her as she reluctantly steps back and allows me to lead her away.

We move through the golden field, letting the sunlight and breeze warm us as we walk. Though, the heat is agonizing for me, I do not let it show.

Silence stretches between us as she twirls to soak it all in, her smile never once melting from her face.

Watching her, I wish I had thought to bring her here sooner.

Guilt twists my stomach as I realize I have been no

better than those before me. I have kept her trapped in the cold confines of my palace, forced to spend her last days alone with nothing but her paints for comfort.

My selfishness, my fear of her effect on me, has made me act with cruelty. Though I know she would never complain, I hate how little I have done to make her happy.

I will not make this mistake again.

For as long as she is here, for as long as I am able, I swear to make every last moment that she has left count.

She will never want for anything again, as long as I can give it to her.

"I have prepared a picnic for us," I say, leading her up a small hill through the tall grass. We stop beneath the shade of a large apple tree, the blanket I laid out earlier already waiting for us.

Knax trots closer, bending to graze near the bottom of the hill. Hazel turns slowly to look out over the valley before turning her attention toward the picnic.

"It looks wonderful," she says enthusiastically. "Thank you."

I clear my throat uncomfortably, but do not voice my own concerns over the collection of cheese, jams, olives, and other items I pulled at random from the kitchen.

Offering my hand, I help her down onto the blanket before joining her.

I watch as she reaches for a slice of bread, liberally spreading bright orange jam over it before taking a bite. Relief washes over me as a sigh of delight escapes her.

"I don't think anyone has ever prepared a picnic specifically for me before."

"I must admit, I am unfamiliar with the customs of mortals," I say. "I was unsure of what exactly I should bring."

"You did excellently," she says with a soft smile.

I doubt that is the truth, but I appreciate the warmth in her voice, and we fall back into silence as she eats.

Her eyes wander across the field before landing on Knax. For several moments we watch as he prances about, clearly showing off for this mortal. It seems that she has managed to win him over in almost no time at all.

"Might I ride him?"

I frown at her simple request.

"No. It is not possible, I am afraid."

"What do you mean?"

"Though you can touch him, it is impossible for any living thing to mount him."

My words take a moment to sink in, but when they do, I feel her curious gaze settle on me.

I realize that I have revealed more to her than I meant to.

Yet, I do not seem to mind.

Not when her entire attention is focused on me, her head tilted to the side as if trying to piece together what I am not explicitly telling her.

Eventually, she asks, "Are you not living then?"

I contemplate how to answer for a long moment.

Part of me wants to explain everything to her. There is a strange desire buried deep within me for her to understand what I am, but I am not sure if I can indulge that part of me.

There are still limits to what I should share with a mortal. Even one marked for death, such as herself.

"It is different," I finally say. "I am neither living nor dead. I simply … am."

She frowns at this before asking, "What meaning is life then, if there is no death awaiting you at the end of it?"

I am quiet for so long that, before I can think of a way to answer, a small laugh escapes her.

She shakes her head; her seriousness disappearing with a soft breeze.

Her eyes still burn bright with curiosity, as though she intends to figure me out eventually. I am not sure why the thought of her doing just that does not terrify me as I know it should.

"You are quite the enigma," Hazel says quietly, looking at me as if she can see straight through my mask.

"Am I?"

"At least when it comes to your state of existence. How can one not be alive but also not be dead? Are you mortal and immortal, too?"

"I suppose one could say that," I answer, and she shakes her head once more.

Her gaze returns to Knax, and I cannot help but feel a little relieved that this particular conversation has ended. At least, for the time being.

I want to tell her everything, to lay myself bare before her, but it is a desire I do not know that I can give into. If more for my sake, than hers.

"Will you walk with me?" she asks, standing to brush the crumbs from her dress.

It is an offer I cannot refuse, and I rise to join her. I offer my arm to her, and I am rewarded with another smile as she slips her arm through mine.

The heat of her touch burns me, but I do not allow myself to shrink away from it. I allow the scorching pain to etch itself into my memory, tattooing her very essence into mine. I savor it, praying that it will never leave me, and abandoning all hope that I might one day forget the havoc she is now wreaking upon my heart.

Might forget that she can never be mine.

The rest of the day passes in a haze as I fill my mind with moments spent with her.

We walk leisurely through the fields, Hazel running her hands through the tall grass and stopping to pick wildflowers. She makes a crown of them, twisting them together before setting it atop her head.

I find myself smiling behind my mask as my eyes catch on it, watching her spin before moving to run a hand over Knax. As the daylight slips away, Knax only seems to grow more fond of Hazel, nudging her playfully with his nose before trotting off before she can reach for him again.

It is only when I see Hazel trying to hide a yawn that I realize it is time for us to head back. She does not complain when I suggest it, and I almost think I see a flicker of relief in her face.

Her steps are slower than usual as we make our way back toward the palace, and I find myself tempted to sweep her up into my arms. To cradle her to my chest and give her rest.

But I do not.

Knax trails behind us, neighing softly at our backs as if to beg us to stay for just a little while longer. Stopping short of the mists, Hazel looks up at me, exhaustion nearly as clear as the joy on her face.

"Can we return here?" she asks.

I stare down at her, my heart breaking in my chest.

"Of course, little one," I say. "We can come back as often as you would like."

I find it easy to promise her this, but then I am reminded how short her time is. It will not be long now before she will be but a memory here, and in the dark halls of my palace.

"Thank you," she whispers, her voice tired even as she smiles up at me. A smile that fills me and tears me to pieces.

A smile that soon, I will have to steal from her.

26

HAZEL

After our day spent in the Valley of Death with Knax, I suddenly find my days filled with Death's presence.

At first, I think I'm imagining it when the shadows seem to deepen around me, shifting out of the corner of my eye wherever I go ... but then, I find myself running into Death more and more frequently.

He always acts surprised. Always pretends like he's in the middle of getting ready to leave the palace on important business, but then he *always* asks if he can walk with me.

And I don't refuse him.

He hasn't left the palace since our day together, but I haven't told him that I know this, or *how* I know this.

Not that I would be able to explain it. It's just that, even when he's not by my side, I seem to be able to feel him in the very breath of this place.

And I don't want that to change.

In a matter of days, our mornings have fallen into rhythm with one another.

I wake with a secret smile, knowing that by the time I have bathed and dressed for the day, Death will be waiting to run into me on the way down to the kitchen. He will ask to accompany me, where he will settle on his stool in the corner while I break my fast.

I find myself opening up to him more each day as I tell him about my life before. He listens quietly, rarely partaking in any food himself.

Then, after breakfast, he always asks me the same thing.

How would I like to spend my day?

Most days, I want nothing more than for him to take me down into the Valley of Death to bask in the sunlight and play with Knax, but often, I find myself drawn back to my studio instead.

As much as I enjoy being with Knax and Death, the more time I spend with them, the harder it is to bear the thought of what's to come.

Death always obliges, always insists that I tell him if there's anything I want before turning and disappearing into the dark halls of his palace.

Even as his shadows linger around me.

I try to not dwell on thoughts of him, or the way my heart grows to long for him every moment we're apart.

———————

"How would you like to spend today?"

I glance up at Death, realizing I'd fallen quiet,

248

consumed by my own thoughts. I start to give him my usual answer, but stop short.

"I don't know."

He cocks his head to the side at this before asking, "Then, tell me, what is one thing you have always wanted to do?"

I consider his question for a moment, letting my imagination run wild before reigning it back in.

"I've always wanted someone to take me dancing on ice," I start, "but that would be impossible."

"Why is that?"

"Well, for one thing, I cannot dance, let alone on ice," I laugh.

He watches me quietly before rising from his seat.

"Come."

My brow furrows in question, but I follow him out of the kitchen and through the palace to the entrance of a grand ballroom. Death glances back at me before turning to gesture toward the room.

I stare, wide-eyed, as his shadows burst out to fill the room. Within seconds, the entire room—walls, floor, and even ceiling—has frozen over with frost and ice, sparkling in the dim light of his palace.

Offering his hand to me, I blink at it before tentatively accepting it.

My skin shivers, chills racing up and down my spine as he pulls me to him.

"I can't dance."

"Then, let me dance for you," he whispers, as I lift my eyes to his. "Step on my feet."

I search his masked face for a moment before stepping up onto his black boots. His hand slips around my waist, settling against the small of my back as he carries me into the iced-over ballroom.

We glide effortlessly over the floor, our eyes locked on one another as we dance. My heart races, the breeze from our movements swishing through my skirts and stirring the loose strands of hair around my face.

I can't help but smile, joy filling me near to bursting.

We dance the day away, the hours slipping by as if they were mere seconds. It's only when exhaustion finally weighs on me, and I press my cheek to Death's hard chest that he stills.

"Don't stop," I whisper, another shiver racking my body as his arms momentarily wrap around me to hold me tighter against him.

"You are tired."

"Please."

Death hesitates before lifting me into his arms, continuing our dance even as he tucks me against his chest.

Even as my eyes close and sleep and dreams carry me with him.

I wake shivering hours later, only to realize I'm still in Death's arms. He's holding me, seated on the lounge by the fire in the sitting room as he stares into it.

"Death?"

He starts, blinking before looking down at me.

"Yes, little one?"

"I think I'm ready for bed," I say with a weak smile.

"Of course."

He rises, carrying me out of the room.

"I can walk."

"And I can carry you."

I don't fight him on this, not that I want to. As cold as I feel in his embrace, I would rather freeze than leave his arms.

Reaching my room, Death bends to set me down, only for me to realize I've grown so cold that I can barely move, let alone walk. I cling to him for support as he tries to step back.

"I-I need your help."

Instantly, I'm in his arms again as he crosses the room.

"I am so sorry," he says, leaning over me as he pulls back the furs to carefully arrange me on the bed.

"Don't say that." He pauses, hovering over me as he tilts his head slightly in confusion. "Don't say you're sorry. I had the most wonderful day with you, and I wouldn't trade it for the world."

He doesn't say anything for a long minute, but I see the way his shadows dance around him.

"I am happy you were pleased."

I give him a tired smile as he moves to pull the furs over me.

"Wait," I say, my cheeks flushing with warmth. "Would you mind terribly if I asked you to remove my boots?"

"You may ask me anything within my power, and I would do it."

Settling onto the edge of the bed, I watch as he carefully unlaces them. His gloved hand shifts higher to wrap around my leg as he gently pulls each boot off.

"And my socks, too?" My heart is pounding in my chest as his eyes slowly lift to meet mine. He slides his hand along my leg, dipping his fingers beneath the fabric to allow them to roll down over my feet and off onto the floor.

"And your dress?" he asks, as if reading my mind.

My mouth is dry, my heartbeat deafening in my ears as I will myself to answer him.

"Yes."

Shifting further onto the bed, he leans over me as his eyes dip to take me in.

"Then I do not think you should wear this dress again."

"Why?"

He doesn't answer. Instead, his gaze lifts to mine as his hands reach for the neckline of my dress. Tearing the thick fabric from my body as easily as if it were merely tissue, he pulls it from beneath me and tosses it aside.

Nothing but the thin chemise lies between us, but he doesn't allow his gaze to travel lower. Grabbing the heavy furs, he pulls them over me, covering my modesty as he rises from the bed.

"Good night, Hazel."

Death bows his head once before turning on his heel and striding out of the room, but not before waving at the fire once with his hand, causing the flames to burn even brighter behind him.

The door closes.

"Good night," I whisper into the empty room.

Over the next few days, Death asks me the same question after breakfast, and no matter how I answer, no matter how impossible my request seems, he finds a way to make it happen. Even if I make so much as an offhand remark about something I enjoy, the next thing I know, I find it gifted or waiting for me.

It's hard to miss the care he takes in everything he does for me. How he worries over my comfort and happiness. He's become more than just a welcome companion, he's become a constant one, too.

He always seems to be near, watching over me with those soul-piercing eyes of his that seem to be growing softer and softer with each passing day.

At first, I think I'm imagining things. That he's simply doing his part as host to entertain me, but his presence becomes harder and harder to explain away.

And then, it becomes impossible to ignore the way he touches me. The way his gloved fingers brush against mine, the press of his hand on the small of my back, the tucking of a loose strand of hair behind my ear.

The way my cheeks flush, and a fire bursts to life within me whenever he is around. Or the way that, when I return to my room each night, it's dreams of him and a future that can never be that guide me to sleep.

With each touch, each day spent together, my heart longs to remain in these moments with him forever, and yet, I hardly dare to believe he feels the same way about me.

Even now, I know how foolish I sound. I am merely a

mortal he's promised to care for in her dying days, and he is simply keeping his word.

Besides, our love would only be doomed, if not entirely forbidden.

And yet, I am unable to stop myself from falling for him.

I don't *want* to.

I know how ridiculous I'm being, and this is nothing more than a fantasy, but I allow myself to live it.

I don't even know what Death truly looks like. For all I know, there's nothing behind his mask but shadow and mist.

But I do not care. All that I know, all that I care about, in this moment is that my heart burns brighter for him with each day I spend in his presence.

And with it comes pain.

I see echoes of a future that was never meant to be. A life that I will never lead.

One where I am free to grow old at Death's side.

Sometimes, in these small moments, I see myself in five or ten years, curled up at his side, content and full of life. Other glimpses offer me children and a family of our own, surrounded by laughter and love, and free from the bitterness of fate.

Glimpses into an impossible future, even if I weren't marked for death.

I try to push these from my mind as soon as they appear. I know it's silly to bother myself with such fantasies. Feeding them will only bring pain.

Some nights, when the fantasies become too real, I have

to remind myself that I do not regret this life that I've chosen. It feels wrong to have to constantly remind myself of this as if I'm trying to convince myself of a lie.

I know it was the right thing to do; it was the only thing to do.

Besides, as much as it pains me to admit it, I never would have had this time with Death if I hadn't. Had I not set out to save Father, had I not struck a deal with Death, I would not be here.

I would not know how deeply one can love another.

No, I would have instead become the plaything of Lord Payne or Amadeus.

The mere thought sends a chill racing down my spine.

I know that I made the right decision to give up my life in exchange for Father's. There is no regret in my heart about this.

At least, I don't think there is.

"Hazel?"

Blinking, I find myself pulled back to the present as I turn to find Death watching me, concern clear in his eyes.

"Are you well?"

I force a smile to my face, realizing I have no idea how long I was lost in thought.

"Yes, I'm fine," I answer, but his eyes don't leave my face, even as I try to convince myself that it's the truth.

"Are you sure, little one?"

In all honesty, I don't feel fine.

I haven't felt fine since just before we visited Knax and the Valley of Death. I had thought I was merely exhausted from painting, but my energy has yet to return.

In fact, it only seems to wane more with each day that passes.

My mind, too, seems to slip from my grasp more frequently now, returning to past memories or dwelling on futures that will never be. Sometimes, I've even found it difficult to distinguish between what is my imagination and what is reality.

I've done my best to hide these changes from Death, but I know it's a losing battle. Sooner or later, he will know, if he doesn't already from the way he hovers. The way he catches my hand when my feet catch on my skirts, the way he insists on carrying me up the stairs when I tell him I'm ready for bed each night.

If I didn't know better, it would be all too easy to convince myself of his love for me. That he loves me as deeply as I've started to love him.

Tilting my head as I trace the outline of his silhouette against the golden field, I snort softly to myself.

Why shouldn't I pretend that he loves me? He never has to know, and I can die happily living out my fantasy.

Pretending that I'm spending the last of my days in the arms of love.

It doesn't take much effort to pretend that we are truly together, lost in one another and the happiness that we find in each other's presence.

I don't care that it's nothing more than a silly daydream.

If nothing else, it will be a lovely way to spend the last of my days here.

"Yes, I'm sure."

Death's gaze finally shifts away to watch Knax whinny and prance about, but his hand remains on my knee.

I stare at his gloved hand, and a smile warms my heart as I realize just how easy my make-believe will be.

27

HAZEL

Leaning back from my easel, I smile. It's perfect.

It's *finally* perfect.

It's taken me the better part of three days to bring my vision to life. Three days spent without Death by my side.

I'd grown so used to him being here that when he actually bid me farewell and stepped out into the swirling mists, it felt like my heart went with him.

Unable to pass the time before his return quickly enough, I soon found myself sitting before my easel.

At least here, in my little studio, I can get lost in the paints, even if the brushes now tremble in my hands.

My eyes move over the painting, a small reminder of our time in the Valley of Death, Knax prancing through the golden fields.

I think I will hang this one in my room. I frown slightly, wondering if Death will keep my paintings or hide them away once I'm gone.

Pushing this morbid thought from my mind, I grab the painting, replacing it on my easel with another, before I head for the door.

Stepping out, something crinkles beneath my foot. Glancing down, I find a small black envelope with my name in beautiful gold lettering.

Bending, I pick it up and carefully open it to read the note tucked away inside.

Hazel,
Wear my favorite dress, and join me downstairs for dinner.
-D

I smile, though part of me questions why I hadn't noticed his return earlier. Leaning against the wall, I make my way back to my room as quickly as I can.

The shadows in the hall are growing long, pushing me to hurry. I don't want to leave Death waiting a moment longer than necessary, especially after not seeing him for so many days.

Back in my room, I place the painting above the fireplace, pleased with the warmth it adds.

Bathing, I wash away the days spent painting before stepping over to my wardrobe. I run hands over the beautiful dresses within before pulling out the one Death mentioned.

Of course, his favorite is the one made from that impossible fabric ... Fabric as black as wet ink and as ethereal as a starry night sky.

It's my favorite dress too, even if it leaves me feeling

chilled to the bone.

Admiring my reflection in the glossy stone wall, I'm unable to tear my eyes away for a moment before realizing that I need to hurry. Braiding my hair and pinning it, I smile as I leave my bedroom.

As eager as I am to see Death, I have to pause several times to catch my breath as I lean against the cold wall.

Reaching the top of the sweeping staircase, I find Death waiting for me at the bottom, dressed in a suit that fits his frame and demeanor so perfectly that I can't help but stare.

My steps falter as I take in how handsome he looks, his bone mask sharp and fitted in such a way that it *almost* looks like it could be his face. His eyes find mine, and I suddenly have to remind myself to breathe.

"Hazel," he says, my name dripping from his lips like sweet wine.

He climbs the stairs to meet me, offering his hand.

I'm quick to take it, his gloved fingers closing around me as my fire burns to life beneath his icy touch.

"I'm so glad you're back," I say, smiling up at him, perfectly content in this moment.

"As am I."

He leads me to the dining room, where the large table is laden with food.

I stare at it for a long moment, realizing that he's somehow managed to gather all of my favorite foods. From the plum pudding Mother used to make to the stuffed duck I had once during my travels with Father, it is all here.

Everything I've ever told him I enjoyed, or wished I

could taste. Sitting on elegant golden platters, begging me to sample them.

I find I have no words to thank him. I turn toward Death with a smile, but it fades from my lips as I see only sorrow returned in his deep black eyes.

It suddenly hits me what this is. What this meal, this time together means.

It's my last day.

I quickly catch my fading smile before it can slip from my face entirely. Swallowing down the sadness that has settled like a pit in my stomach, I force the cheeriness back to my smile.

I will not allow the heaviness of sorrow to weigh me down. I will not let it drown me. I will not waste my last moments here.

No, I will enjoy this last meal with Death at my side.

Then I will meet my fate with a smile.

I will not allow Death to see me fall apart, not here.

Not now.

There is no point. This is the deal that I made.

I knew this day was coming, and I will not let Father, or Death, down by falling to pieces now.

Death leads me to my seat, before joining me.

Despite the dark thoughts that threaten to tear my heart asunder, I force myself to live in the moment. Together, Death and I dine on all my favorites as well as several new ones. We laugh, sharing happy stories as we eat and commenting on the stranger dishes that we like and dislike.

The food is delicious, and he is wonderful company,

ensuring that my cup is full and I get to sample everything before me. I tell Death of life before Merelda, of Mother, of the happier days of my childhood, and he seems to hang on every word.

Something about this has my mind recalling things I might not have otherwise. Suddenly stopping mid-story, I frown.

"You never did mention if you found that book I lost in the forest."

"No, I suppose I did not."

"Well, did you?"

He hesitates for a second before answering, "No, but I have another gift for you."

I frown as he reaches into his jacket, pausing before changing hands to check the other side. I nearly scream when he places a finger down on the table in front of me.

"What kind of gift is that?!"

He glances between me and the finger silently before shoving his hand back into his pocket and sets a single, snake ring down next to the finger.

I blink at it in shock.

"Lord Payne will never bother you, or any other maiden again."

"What did you do?" I gasp.

"I did not kill him."

"That isn't what I asked."

"I could not, in good conscience, show you the other parts of him I removed."

I hardly know what to say as I stare down at the familiar ring.

"I need you to promise me something," I say, finally dragging my eyes back to Death.

"Anything."

"You will not maim another living person in my life, without first discussing it with me."

His fingers clench into a fist on the table before slowly relaxing.

"Very well," he says. "If that is what you wish."

"It is," I say, before quickly adding, "unless it is in my immediate defense, of course."

"Naturally."

We return to our meal in silence for a few minutes. As my shock wanes, I find myself glancing back up at Death, my heart swelling with love for him. To think that he would be willing to go to such lengths for me, over someone doing me harm.

"Thank you," I say softly.

He nods once before reaching for his gift and tossing it into the nearby fireplace. I smile at him, and we slip quietly back into pleasant conversation.

When the meal is done, he stands and offers me his hand. Wordlessly, I once again slip mine into his.

We say nothing as we leave the dining room behind, and I take one last look back. I can't help but wonder how long those dishes will sit there after I'm gone.

Together, we make our way through the now familiar halls of the palace, and I find myself taking it all in one last time. Sadness threatens to overtake me as I realize how much I will miss this place.

Almost as much as I will miss Death himself

Hand in hand, he leads me once more to the Valley of Death, but as we emerge from the swirling mist, I am stunned to see how different it looks.

I've never been here at night, and somehow, it's even more ethereal beneath the starry sky. The whole valley almost seems to glow in soft dreamy colors, the night air filled with the sweet perfume of flowers.

"Come," Death says as I glance up at him, just as Knax comes thundering toward us, his white coat gleaming in the pale light.

Leading me deeper into the valley, Death suddenly pulls me to his chest, and for a moment I'm lost, until he leans in.

"Dance with me," he says, his deep voice sending another shiver across my skin as I suddenly realize a melody lilts around us, filling the meadow.

I step onto his shoes, and together we dance as Knax prances around us. I lean in, pressing my head to Death's chest, content in this moment together.

We dance beneath the moonless sky until I find myself too tired even to cling to Death. Together we lie back on the thick, soft grass.

"I know tonight is my last," I say quietly, staring up at the pale sky as I feel Death's gaze settle on me.

He says nothing in response.

Turning away from the sky, I glance to him. There is such sorrow in his eyes that my heart clenches.

"When must it happen?" I ask.

"Soon."

"How soon?"

"Before the rays of dawn's first light."

I nod, turning back to watch the strange sky.

"Will you allow me to die here?"

"No," he says, his voice low. "Not here."

Without warning, he rises to lift me into his arms.

Cradling me against his chest, his arms tighten around me as we leave the meadow and Knax behind. I nestle my head against him, fighting back a smile at the way he tenderly carries me through the halls.

It takes me a moment to realize where he's headed. My eyes search his masked face as we step into his bedroom and he places me down gently atop his bed.

My chest pounds in my chest as I gaze up at him. Unable to help myself, I feel hope growing within me as I can only hope where this might be leading.

Our eyes meet, and for a moment, neither of us moves. But then he straightens, icy shadows rushing in to fill the space where he once touched me, as though misreading the excitement in my gaze for something else.

"Do not worry, little one," he tells me. "I did not bring you here to bed you."

"I-I do not understand," I say, trying to keep the disappointment from my voice.

"I thought it only seemed fitting that I take your soul here," he says. "Here, where I will have to live with what I have done to you for the rest of eternity."

"You haven't done anything to me. I chose this. It isn't your fault."

He doesn't answer, as he glances away.

"The time is near."

I watch, my heart thudding painfully in my chest, as he starts to remove one of his gloves.

Unable to stop myself, I reach for him. He pauses, his eyes once more returning to mine. A moment passes before he cocks his head to the side in silent question.

"I have a gift for you, too."

He looks taken aback at this, unsure of what to say to this.

"What gift?"

"A name."

"I am afraid I do not understand."

"I do not want you to take me as Death," I say carefully. "Death is not your name; it is what you are. If you would let me, I would like to give you a name of my own."

He tilts his head to the other side, as if intrigued.

"And what is this name?"

"Sydian."

"What made you choose this name?"

I blush, biting my lip as I look away.

"It seems appropriate to name you after the obsidian you surround yourself with, but I didn't want it to be quite so obvious."

"Sydian," he says, mulling the name over. "Very well, you may call me by this name, but it must only ever be spoken between us."

"Thank you."

"Of course, little one."

He nods once before reaching for his glove again.

"Wait," I say, knowing I'm pushing my luck. "Is it too much to also ask to look upon your face before I die?"

He freezes, his body tense as he watches me.

"Would it please you?"

"Yes," I answer without hesitation.

He nods once, and excitement bubbles within me once more as he reaches for his mask. His fingers dip below the edge, and he hesitates for another moment before slowly removing it.

His dark hair falls in inky waves to frame his face as a gasp escapes me. His face is sharp, all angles and terrifying beauty. It's powerful, strikingly so. His pitch-black eyes further emphasized by thick eyebrows and porcelain skin.

In a way, it's even more frightening than the bone masks he chooses to hide it with.

He's beautiful.

"I am not meant to be beautiful, little one," he says, and I realize that I've spoken aloud. "I am meant to be terrifying."

A small laugh bursts from me at this.

"It is terrifying."

His brow furrows in question as he looks at me, and I savor finally being able to see him do so.

"How do you mean?"

"Your face," I try again. "It's terrifying in its perfection. In its beauty. I could gaze upon it for the rest of my life, and still, I would never be able to replicate its perfection on my canvas."

"Tell me, little one, would you die to look upon this face?"

"Yes," I tell him without hesitation. "A thousand times o—"

I never get to finish my sentence.

His eyes sharpen at my words, and before I know it, he's bent to pull me to him. His lips melt against mine, stealing my very breath away.

My heart soars as I lose myself to his touch, the tender way his lips move against mine. Joy, love, and thrill burst into flames within me as he deepens the kiss, mixing with the icy tendrils of his shadows as they crash over me.

Then just as quickly as these feelings swell within me, they fade into darkness as my soul is pulled from me.

28

DEATH

"No!" I roar into the night, the room filling with darkness as my shadows burst from me before slowly crawling back.

My hands shake as I stare down at her, too late, realizing what I have just done. I find myself unable to look away as my eyes trace over the soft smile on her lips, the light gone from her eyes.

A single tear rolls down her cheek breaking, as the room fills with the silence. The song of her soul gone from me as I hold her limp, lifeless body in my arms.

My heart shatters into a million pieces.

Our deal is complete.

I lost myself in my desire for her, and because of that, I sealed her fate with a kiss.

A kiss that silenced the words I meant to speak. Words that I have long wished to tell her.

Words that I know she could never return.

And now, she has died, never knowing how deeply I loved her.

How much I love her still.

Gently, I lay her back against my pillows.

I take in her soft beauty for a long moment before rising.

Storming from my room, anger burns through me as I struggle to come to terms with what I have just done.

I know that I will have to return her body to the mortal realm before long.

But I cannot, not yet.

Not now.

I am not ready for her to be gone from this place.

I make my way toward the main entrance of my palace, ready to unleash my vengeance upon the world. Rage builds within me, my shadows storming about me as my steps echo through the halls.

When I suddenly notice an open door.

Hazel's studio.

Pain stabs my heart, but I am unable to stop myself as I turn toward it.

Stepping into the room, my stomach knots as I glance about the empty space before my eyes settle on the canvas set in the middle of the room.

It is the portrait she painted of me.

Only she has changed it.

No longer am I alone on the canvas. Next to me, stands a tiny version of herself, smiling and shining as brightly as she did in life.

A portrait of us.

Moving toward it, I search each brush stroke, seeking out the small pieces of herself that she poured into this painting.

I feel it, then.

Her love for me. Nearly as overwhelming as mine in its intensity.

My heart stings as everything else fades away, and I fall to my knees before it as I roar in anguish.

I allow myself a few moments to collect myself again, slowly rising to my feet before turning on my heel.

I will find a way to bring her soul back.

I will do whatever it takes to save her, even if that means I must defy all of the Underworld to do it.

Even if I must go against the Fates themselves.

THANK YOU

Thank you for reading *Kiss of Death*, the first book in the *Tempting the Fates* series.

If you enjoyed this book ...

You can stay up to date on upcoming new releases in this series and others by following Alice Wilde on **Amazon**, **Facebook**, Instagram, or Tiktok, or by signing up for her newsletter at alicewilde.com.

If you would recommend this book, or others by Alice Wilde, please consider leaving a review on Amazon or reaching out to let her know!

ALSO BY ALICE WILDE

Tempting the Fates

Kiss of Death

Touch of Death

Until Death

Love and Death

A Kingdom of Wolves

Of Wolves and Women

Of Wolves and Warriors

Of Wolves and Wives

A Deal with the Devils

The Vampire's Deal

The Vampire's Maiden

The Vampire's Vow

Fated to the Alphas

Alpha Forsaken

Alpha Marked

Alpha Claimed

Alpha Bound

The White Wolf Trilogy

ABOUT THE AUTHOR

Alice Wilde works as a full-time game editor, graphic designer, and, most importantly, author.

She loves creating paranormal, fantasy romances full of gorgeous men, magic, twists, and cliffhangers that she hopes her readers enjoy reading as much as she enjoys writing them.

Alice currently lives in Asia with her cat dreaming up, writing down, and living in her next book alongside her characters ...

Follow Alice Wilde on Facebook/ Amazon to stay up to date with new releases.

CONNECT WITH ALICE

EMAIL: **alicewildeauthor@gmail.com**

TIKTOK: @ALICEWILDEAUTHOR

facebook.com/AliceWildeAuthor

instagram.com/alice_wilde_author

Made in the USA
Columbia, SC
12 June 2025

59321319R00171